Walking the Maze

OTHER OXFORD FICTION

The Scavenger's Tale
Rachel Anderson

The War Orphan
Rachel Anderson

Against the Day
Michael Cronin

Shadows
Tim Bowler

The Throttlepenny Murder
Roger J. Green

Witchy
Ann Phillips

The Eagle of the Ninth
Rosemary Sutcliff

Walking the Maze

Margret Shaw

OXFORD
UNIVERSITY PRESS

OXFORD
UNIVERSITY PRESS

Great Clarendon Street, Oxford OX2 6DP

Oxford University Press is a department of the University of Oxford.
It furthers the University's objective of excellence in research, scholarship,
and education by publishing worldwide in

Oxford New York

Athens Auckland Bangkok Bogotá Buenos Aires Calcutta
Cape Town Chennai Dar es Salaam Delhi Florence Hong Kong Istanbul
Karachi Kuala Lumpur Madrid Melbourne Mexico City Mumbai
Nairobi Paris São Paulo Singapore Taipei Tokyo Toronto Warsaw

and associated companies in Berlin Ibadan

Oxford is a registered trade mark of Oxford University Press
in the UK and in certain other countries

British Library Cataloguing in Publication Data available

ISBN 0 19 275094 1

1 3 5 7 9 10 8 6 4 2

Typeset by AFS Image Setters Ltd, Glasgow

Printed in Great Britain

The ancient mazes of England were used by maidens to test their suitors. The maiden would stand at the centre, which was called 'Home', and call upon her sweetheart to walk the maze and bring her out.

Mrs Campbell mistrusted the printed word, for all books are subversive and all writers are revolutionaries.

She looked down at the billowing hedges, twenty-five feet high and bellied with age, past the lily pond with its fairy statue, to where the lawn ended and the meadow began. The line between cultivation and chaos was a thin wire fence, invisible to the eye.

Mrs Campbell settled her straw hat more firmly on her head. The trouble with Annice, she began to say to herself, and then she stopped and stared at the book beside her, the book that had, above all others, brought about what she called 'my daughter's spot of bother'. It looked harmless enough—*Naturalists both Amateur and Mercenary*—a book about gardens and flowers, a kind, soothing, old fashioned subject. But that, Mrs Campbell thought, that was how they sucked you in.

She opened it at the bookmark and read.

'A path runs crookedly from the gate and . . .'

1

*. . . and leads enticingly from flowers, to lawn, to
pond, to shrubbery, to orchard.*

I am Annice Campbell. I am sure of this. I know this,
although I am not so sure where I am or even when I
am. What do I know for certain?

I know that tears are running down, stinging my
upper lip which is stiff with blood and mucus. I know
that my legs are a tartan of bruises, scratches, and cuts
and my left arm looks odd. It is probably broken. At
some time recently I have been sick. I am surprised by
this for I have not eaten for so long. I have run and run
and can run no more. I must think. I must remember.

It began simply enough. I saw the Wolsingtons for the first
time just after my fifteenth birthday. I was not looking
for them, not expecting them. I suppose that I had fallen
into the habit of expecting very little.

It was a cold day in November and I was once again
in a new town which was my father's doing and in a
gallery of modern art which was my mother's. It had
been decided by then that I was artistic. I accepted this
because I was not much good at anything else. I liked to
read but not to talk about my reading and certainly not
to write about it and I regarded team games as a sinful
waste of time.

The trouble with Annice, they said, is that she lacks
self-discipline. The trouble with Annice, they said, is

that she has a creative temperament. The trouble with Annice is that she is a high flyer. The trouble with Annice is that she is a gadfly. It depended on the point of view.

My mother was in the gallery shop buying postcards. She and the sales girl were talking as though they had known each other for a long time and I was irritated. I disliked the way that she talked with anyone and everyone. We could not get on a bus, or sit in a park, or go to a library without conversations. My mother's interest in people was promiscuous; I liked to think that mine was fastidious.

Over the years I had developed a technique for galleries. I walked quickly from room to room letting the pictures glide past, looking at nothing directly. If something caught my eye I would stop and stare at it. In rooms where the paintings were dull it was the brash and the violent that stopped my progress, in rooms where the paintings were cheerful it was the monotone that arrested me. Then I moved back and forth from the chosen picture as though studying brushwork and effects. I hoped that this made other visitors think that I was an expert, familiar with the place, that I belonged. On that day, however, I wandered aimlessly, my mind too clogged with thoughts to play even this simple game.

I was about to start a new school yet again and I knew that I was unlikely to be thought an asset.

'So I'm afraid that Annice must leave,' my mother told my last headmistress.

'Such a shame,' the headmistress said.

'Annice Campbell is leaving,' the headmistress told my form teacher. And then asked, 'Which one is she?'

'Annice is moving north with her family,' my form mistress told the class.

They smiled politely and without interest. This was

not surprising, I had been in the school only two terms. I had been at the school before that for almost a year, and the one before that nearly two years. The longest that I had been anywhere was the three years between my fifth and eighth birthdays. I fancied that it was then that I was happiest. We had stayed so long in that place because my father was teaching, not 'working'. He taught when he could not find real work. Teaching was a job. His 'work' was something else.

I came to the last room in the art gallery. It was a partition, strangely proportioned, little more than a very high corridor, but with a window that filled the whole of one side. Work was still going on in the room for there were boxes piled at one end and canvases standing on the floor with their faces turned to the walls. In a corner was a pile of dusty sheets.

Only two pictures had been hung so far. They were placed side by side. One was a painting of a group of people standing before the bare wall of a house. They stood in a desolation of bare brown, though in the distance could be seen a brilliantly green landscape. The line between the two was abrupt and artificial. This painting was titled 'Caffelmeade'. The other picture was a photograph of a painting. In it a group of people stood before the wall of a house which was covered in a Virginia creeper and around them was a crowded, lusciously overgrown garden. This one was called 'The Birthday Party'. There was a note at the side.

> *'The Birthday Party' was painted by F. Bennett in 1984 to celebrate Flora Wolsington's sixteenth birthday. In 1994 Bennett painted over the original to produce 'Caffelmeade'.*

I did not wonder why the artist had done such a thing, not then. I looked up to the fanlight thirty feet

4

above and kept my eyes open to the brightness as long as I could. Then I turned to the window. There was a giant oak bare of leaves but with a few withered acorns still clinging. I turned back to the painting and . . . and nothing. Nothing happened. I want to make that very clear. There was nothing on this first visit to suggest that a chain of events had been started that would blow my world apart, would change how I look at, well, how I look at everything. I did not realize it, there was nothing to warn me.

2

I know a bank where the wild thyme [Thymus
serpyllum] *blows,*
Where oxlips [Primula elatior] *and the nodding
violet* [Viola riviniana] *grows,*
Quite over-canopied with lush woodbine [Lonicera
periclymenum],
With sweet musk-roses [Rosa moschata], *and with
eglantine* [Rosa rubiginosa]
        A Midsummer Night's Dream (Act 2, *Scene I*)

I realize now that I probably had a chance on the very next day to change what was to happen, but of course I did not know it then.

'Do I look all right?'

My mother twirled on her slender heels so that I could check her over. Neat navy skirt, a tailored jacket that said 'serious', and a soft white blouse that said 'feminine'. She lifted and fluffed out her hair with her hands, the nails, expertly lacquered in smart scarlet, slid through the curls, dark red and salon-streaked with gold. Her make-up was porcelain perfect. I nodded.

'First impressions matter—'

I nodded again and finished the sentence silently with her:

'—a temporary secretary does not mean a casual secretary.'

'I hope that I get an interesting assignment. Not the first

6

one, of course. I can't expect the first to be interesting, but by the end of the week . . .'

Suddenly I realized that my mother disliked moving about the world as much as I did; hated changing jobs, as much as I hated changing schools. The thought had not occurred to me before and I was shaken because if I had not known this what else might I not know?

'Perhaps we'll be able to stay here longer,' I said encouragingly. 'Manchester's a big city. Perhaps the show will run for ever or maybe Dad'll get more work right here.'

My mother looked uncertain but said, 'Maybe, dear.'

'This is a bigger theatre than the last one anyway,' I added.

'A bit,' she conceded but we both knew that even large theatres went dark.

Once my mother had gone I made a pot of coffee and poured it into a vacuum jug. I carried it up to the first floor of our new home, turning sideways on the narrow stairs. My father had taken over the front bedroom of the little terraced house. His desk was in the middle of the floor. It was clear except for a tier of wire baskets, a telephone, and a clean blotter placed in the exact centre. The rest of the room was cluttered with all manner of bric-a-brac, and models of theatre sets were suspended on strings from the rafters. He was sitting at his drawing board, his fingers clenched round a pencil, his eyes only inches from the paper. He was doing fine, precise work, the pencil moving purposefully but only in a tiny area.

'I've made you some coffee,' I said.

He looked at me uncertainly. I sometimes wondered if he truly remembered me. It was as though he was reminded of me whenever I spoke and was surprised to find that I was still there.

'Thank you,' he said. 'That was a kind thought.'

7

'What are you doing?'

'Come and look. It's *The Dream*.'

I looked at the drawing. It was a dense garden crowded with fantastic botanically impossible flowers and threatening heavy foliage. The weight of greens was centrally torn by a light airy clearing in the palest of blue and white. Here strange animals could be seen. Elephants whose proportions were not quite right, giraffes with etoliated necks like plants kept in the dark, rhinoceroses with too long horns, alligators with quick little legs, insects as big as pigs, and pigs as luminous as neon. All my father's stage sets were cramped fantasies, impossible to build and with no room for the actors.

'It will take a lot of flats and flies,' I said.

'We could use gauzes,' he suggested.

'Are you doing *A Midsummer Night's Dream* then?' I asked.

'What?'

'Is that what the theatre's going to do?'

'Oh! No. I don't expect so,' he replied. 'After the pantomime they will have to do something a bit more commercial than Shakespeare.'

'Then why?'

'Why what?'

'Why *A Midsummer Night's Dream*?'

'Why not? It gives the imagination scope.' He frowned. 'Don't look like that, Annice.'

'Like what?'

'Disapproving and knowing at the same time.'

'I'm sorry. I didn't realize that that's how I looked.'

He waited and then said, 'But?'

'What?'

'There's always a "but".'

'But this isn't how *A Midsummer Night's Dream* looked,' I told him.

8

'I know I'll regret this,' he sighed, 'but why not?'

'Shakespeare was very precise. "I know a bank where the wild thyme" and all that. You can put botanical names to his plants. They're not fantastical. They're real—thyme, oxlip, musk rose, eglantine, woodbine— they're all English flowers known since the earliest records.'

'So Shakespeare was a botanist as well?'

'I didn't say that.'

'But?'

'But he knew his plants.'

My father raised his eyebrows and shook his head.

'Just how do you know these things, Annice?'

'I read it somewhere. In one of your books, I think.'

'Even so,' he said, 'this is my *Midsummer Night's Dream*. I'm allowed to interpret a bit, I suppose?'

I shrugged. 'I suppose so. Do you think that it will ever get made?'

'It doesn't matter if it doesn't.'

'But you pretend that it will, don't you?'

'Everyone pretends a bit. That's how we invent ourselves.'

'I don't!'

'But then you hardly know you're born yet.'

I tried to frame an answer but he had already gone back to work.

'Are you going to the theatre today?' I asked.

'Yes. Later.'

'Right.'

'Are you going to . . .' He was already drawing again and his sentence trailed off.

'School,' I finished for him. 'No. I start school tomorrow.'

'That's good. Best get going then, you don't want to be late on your first day. I hope that you like it.'

As I went on up the stairs I heard the telephone ring and my father answered it. His voice was crisp, certain, decisive. Not for the first time I wondered why he was so attentive to colleagues and so careless of me. As I stumped as noisily as I could on the treads, I told myself how badly I was treated. Thump on the first step, he never really listened to me. Thud on the second step, he was miserly with his time, doling it out in short lengths. Smack on the third step, he treated me like a household pet to be fondled as and when needed. Bang on the fourth step, he would have done better with a cat.

I was to live in the attic. The roof sloped down to the floor at one side and I had stuffed this area with books, lying them on their backs in piles. I could only get at them by lying on my stomach. There was about two metres of space in the middle of the room where I could stand upright and a skylight at the very highest point. I stood on a chair and put my head and shoulders through and looked out at the city.

I had a day to kill.

'You shouldn't wish your life away.' But what else could I do with it, alone in a strange place?

The house was one of a row of four mill-workers' cottages that had been left right in the middle of the city. There had once been hundreds of such houses but the heavy ball of the developer had swung against those that the German bombs had missed and that had not sunk into the Victorian sewers. This row had been saved for sentiment and instruction and now had a preservation order on it. This meant that the houses could be lived in but not altered. Because the poky low windows had to stay and garages could not be added, they were cheap even though they were right beside the shops, the theatres, the colleges, and the offices. This meant that my parents could afford to live there.

I went back down the stairs. I switched on the TV. I sat down. I stood up. I switched off the TV. I got a magazine and flung myself on to the sofa. Books never let me down. I do not remember learning to read. I do not remember a time when I could not read. I read mechanically even before I could understand the individual words. Amongst my earliest words were 'riboflavin' and 'monosodiumglutamate'. Lovely words. There was something soothing about the very act of reading. I read and at some level absorbed books that were way beyond my understanding, finishing *Pride and Prejudice* before I was ten and ruining Jane Austen for myself forever. But even I drew the line at the *Woman's Daily Chat*. I flung the magazine down. I stood up and plumped the cushion.

If I put my hand on the sitting room wall and stretched out the other I only had to take three sideways steps and I was through the door and touching the wall in the hall. That was the entire width of our home. I took the first coat that came to hand and went out.

The front door opened straight on to the street, across which was a carpark and an assortment of lock-up sheds and workshops. It was scruffy, but at least it was of human proportion, whereas the back door went to a small yard overshadowed by the blank side of a tower block that belonged to the university.

It was cold and the rain was falling half-heartedly; not proper splashy drops, just persistent wetness. I put the coat on and discovered that it was my father's long, waxed drover's coat. It reached my feet and the shoulders drooped dispiritedly. I belted it tightly and shoved the sleeves as far up as they would go. If I plunged my hands into the pockets it wasn't too bad and with the collar turned up only the very top of my head would get wet.

So this is Manchester, I thought. The damp air palely loitered around the glassy red Victorian brick, around the heavy grey stone, shining like pewter, around the slender steel and glass rocket towers. Manchester loomed. It was bulbously grey and lumpily luminous in the fog like a misshapen baroque pearl. Tucked between a fast-food outlet and a shoe shop was an old inn, its sign hanging limply like washing on a wet day. On it, a man in black with a magnifying glass bent over a meadow over which were scattered primitive drawings of plants. 'The Amateur Naturalist'. I pulled the book out of my father's pocket. *Naturalists both Amateur and Mercenary*. I smiled because I liked coincidences and I wondered what a mercenary naturalist might be. A man with a gun and a flower press? A man with a grenade and a butterfly net? A man with . . .

I found myself at the gallery without ever admitting to myself that that was where I was going, though I knew once I went through the door that I had come to look at the pictures again. There was nobody there except the woman in the shop and the attendants who were sitting on their chairs lost in newspapers. I pretended to look at other pictures but it was just a game because I knew that eventually I would go into the room at the end.

I stood before the photograph of the birthday party and saw that the Wolsingtons were in fancy dress. They were not clothes of any particular time, not proper costumes, just the odd assortment that people keep for dressing up. The man wore a shirt with white tabbed collar and black tailcoat and breeches with silver buckles. He might be a preacher of some kind. The woman had a long-sleeved blouse fastened primly to the neck with a cameo brooch and a heavy long skirt either pleated or perhaps divided. The girl was draped in a

12

piece of muslin that might have been a curtain. It was caught beneath her bosom with ribbons and her hair was tied untidily on top of her head. The boy was in a white shirt and trousers, the only concession to dressing up was a loosely tied cravat. The little girl, who looked about five years old, was wearing a miniature Japanese kimono in fuschia pink, complete with cushioned belt.

I turned to the painting and realized that it was not only the setting that had been painted over, for the people had also been brought up to date. The man still wore black but now it was jeans and the white collar was now part of a sweatshirt. His hair was speckled with grey. The woman's blouse was now open at the throat and the divided skirt had been slimmed down into trousers. Her hair was less red, her skin more transparent, her eyes less clear. The girl had changed the most. It was still the girl in the muslin, but she was now a mature woman and the dress was a more opaque yellow.

I felt uneasy about the transformations. I looked again at the girl in the photograph and then at the woman she had become in the painting. It was frightening, almost like seeing a loved and trusted face change to hate or evil. The hair lifted on the back of my neck and I was sweating but cold. Perhaps I should have walked away then.

I turned to the window. The rain was now falling fast, melting the giant oak into rivulets of black, grey, and brown. I turned back quickly as though I might surprise the Wolsingtons in some way, but they still looked out steadily from the paper and from the canvas. It was then that I knew that something was very wrong. Although the man, the woman, and the girl had been aged by the artist, the boy had hardly changed at all. He was only slightly different in that the cravat was gone and he now wore an open-necked shirt. Surely, I reckoned, ten years? Surely he should by now be a grown man? Then I looked at the little girl and my heart seemed to stop and then resume beating painfully at my ribcage, for I saw that the child had not changed at all, she was still grinning widely from the Japanese silk folds, still about five years old.

I could, I suppose, have left and never gone back but I think that it was probably too late even then.

3

In the eighteenth century hybridization was tested by
applying the pollen of a carnation (Dianthus
caryophyllus) *to the stigma of a sweet william*
(Dianthus barbatus). *The result, a large double red*
flower, was found to be infertile.

That evening I pinned the postcards that I had bought at the gallery to my wall so that I could see them whilst lying in bed. A church clock began to toll. Six o'clock. My mother would be home soon. Bong. Bong. Bong. If I crossed my eyes I could almost impose one on top of the other, 'Caffelmeade' on 'The Birthday Party', but it made me dizzy and the room dissolved into whiteness. Dissolve is not the right word for it did not happen gradually. The room was there. Then it was not. Neither is white the right word, for it was not white like fog or snow, for nothing moved in the pure brightness. It was not like falling asleep. I was everywhere, there was nothing that was not me, while at the same time I had contracted to a single point. For an unknown amount of time, a moment but also an eternity, I only existed as an idea of myself.

The sun beat down on my head and I felt slightly sick. I narrowed my eyes against the glare and tried to see where I was. This was only a formality really, because I knew where I was with absolute certainty. I was at Caffelmeade and it was late summer.

The garden was full of itself, cramped with leaves,

15

heavy with flowers, weighted with fruit. There was no air in the pathways, no space between the vegetation, no light through the branches. It was controlled wildness, disciplined profusion, as close and as abundant as a William Morris wallpaper. It was at its best. It was what it was for.

I turned through what had been imposing gateposts, but the gates were rusty and off their hinges, propped back on crumbling bricks. The door of the lodge hung slackly open, the unglazed windows were blind, the York-stone tiles, missing in patches, revealed the wooden skeleton. Ahead of me ancient horse-chestnuts lined the drive. They met overhead, cutting out the sun.

'Last night I dreamt I went to Manderley again.'

I went into this living tunnel, the cold descending, enclosing, pressing. I was walking quite naturally and could feel the grit through the soles of my shoes. Occasionally the sun broke through where trees were beginning to die, their limbs disgracefully and pathetically unclothed.

'They'll be gone in ten years.'

Someone had said that to me but I could not remember who or when.

I broke free of the trees and there was Caffelmeade almost immediately on top of me. The parkland had prepared me for its size but not for its ugliness. It was a portly redbrick Tudor house, with an elaborately metalled door and dully glazed windows, top-heavy with chimneys, charmless.

I was now passing a ten foot high wall of ancient crumbling brick. There was a gate made of individual planks on which was painted a crude picture of fields, hedges, and sky. It had rotted in places and the dark holes made clouds in the blue. I went through the gate and found myself on a short gravel path set at right

16

angles to a wider one. It was not a mysterious garden, no secret places, hidden dells or narrow pathways. It would be easy for me to invent this, to egg the pudding, to tell you a fairytale, to fool you. I have fooled others. I have fooled myself too. In honesty I saw an English garden, like other English gardens, showing an open friendly face.

I was halfway down a wide path which ran straight and true from the terrace of the house. Down each side of the path were deep herbaceous borders in their full summer profusion. I could hear voices, slow easy conversation. I had only two choices, right towards the house or left towards the voices in the garden.

I set off towards the voices. The flowers rose high above me on each side and I felt like Moses parting the Red Sea. The billowing waves of asters, lilies, poppies, hollyhocks, and delphiniums crowded the borders, breaking every so often into the white froth of gypsophila. I stopped by a clump of tall yellow flowers that I did not recognize. A breeze came from nowhere and bent the spikes horizontally towards me and I was in an instant blinded by pollen. Nothing else in the garden stirred.

> 'Each little flower that opens,
> Each little bird that sings . . .'

I turned towards the singing, rubbing my eyes. A tall but frail old man was moving amongst the flowers. His head was bald but the white hair which remained around his neck was long and straggled sparsely on to his narrow shoulders. He was wearing close-fitting black apart from a canvas apron that was wrapped many times around his waist. As he moved, arthritis bent his knees, elbows, and wrists at sharp angles so that he looked like a cranefly flittering amongst the blooms, landing lightly, and flittering off again.

'He made their glowing colours
He made their tiny wings . . .'

He held a paintbrush in one hand and a glass jar in the other. He tickled a flower, holding the glass over the brush whilst he moved and then painted another bloom. He did this over and over as I peered through the welling tears.

'Excuse me,' I said.

The gardener stopped in mid-stoop as though frozen, then he turned cautiously and I saw that he was wearing a clerical collar. He did not answer but began singing again and dusting the flowers.

'All things bright and beautiful . . .'

'Excuse me,' I began again, 'I don't seem to know why I'm here. I'm sure I'll remember in a minute, but . . .'

This time the old man stopped in such a difficult position that he fell right over. I moved towards him but was imperiously admonished.

'Don't come on to the flowers, young woman, I'm quite all right.'

And in truth he was again standing, although I had not seen him get up. None of the plants beneath him had been crushed. He resumed his work.

'Do you mind telling me what you are doing?' I asked.

'Hybridization. Do you know that word?'

'Yes.'

'Do you now? That's interesting. Are you a plantsman yourself?'

'No. I don't think that we have a garden,' I said. I seemed to remember a yard with a concrete floor and some broken plantpots with dispirited stalks in them, but the memory was quickly gone.

'No garden? Oh, that's a pity! Well, I'm trying to

cross this carnation with this sweet william. A few years ago I thought that I had succeeded for there were a few hybrids about, but there aren't any now. They must have been barren. That's the trouble. They're often mules.'

He peered at me and noticed my swollen eyes.

'You don't look very happy. Want to help me? We have a duty to control the wilderness or it will overpower us. I am the hand of God.'

'Overpowered by flowers?'

'Look at that wall, young woman. Do you see how it is cracked and buckled and how it begins to crumble? Could you do that without tools?'

I shook my head.

'A tender little plant, a wild geranium, can. Look, it has forced its way through three feet of foundations and displaced the bricks. That's strength.'

The clergyman removed his glasses and cleaned them on an outsize handkerchief. The edges of his black legs and arms waved in the haze as though melting in the heat. As he resettled his spectacles he reformed solidly.

I rubbed my eyes.

'What's wrong with you? You seem to be forever crying.'

'I've got pollen in my eyes.'

'Which flowers?'

I pointed to the tall yellow spikes.

'The asphodel?' The old man smiled but there was sadness in the smile. 'No wonder you don't know where you are,' he said.

'I'll remember in a minute,' I said blinking.

He nodded kindly.

'That's right, dear. I'm sure you will. The others are in the maze.'

A long black arm was stretched out and a knobbled finger pointed.

19

'Goodbye,' I called over my shoulder.
The gardener made no reply.

> 'The cold wind in the winter
> The pleasant summer sun . . .'

I turned back, but the Hand of God had gone. The border was undisturbed. I could not even see where the old man had fallen. It seemed to me that the sweet williams in that area were larger, frillier, and of a deeper colour.

I went through a clipped privet arch and into the maze. The hedges were five feet high which meant that I would have had to jump to see over, but there was no need for I walked to the centre as though I knew the way, and there they were, arranged as though for a painting. I had already seen them in a painting, in two paintings. In spite of all that followed, this is how I will for ever see them.

The woman stood perfectly still as though listening intently. She had a jug of lemonade in her hand. I had seen nothing like her except in an illustrated Tennyson. She was nearly six feet tall, and wore her abundant hair, the colour of burnt toffee, in an unfashionable knot at the nape of her neck.

Her daughter, there was no mistaking the fact that she was her daughter, though her red hair was cut shorter and she wore a cropped top and shorts, was draped over a deckchair with a sketch pad on her lap. From time to time she drew, but mostly she stared foolishly into the sun or blankly at the gravel path. She was near enough my own age but very different from me. Although she was hardly moving, a halo of energy shone about her, trapped power, like a big cat. I recognized the stuff that heroines are made from.

The boy sat on the grass in front of the deckchair. He was all the country heroes in all the books. He was John Ridd, he was Gabriel Oak, he was Mellors. I had always thought of my father as fair, but now I had a different yardstick.

> *'O brave new world*
> *That has such people in't.'*

The girl was not looking at him but her swinging foot tapped him gently on the shoulder.

The man from the paintings was shaping the inner circular hedge, clippings growing around his feet as he worked.

The little girl lay on her back with the cat crouched beneath the squat pyramid made by her chubby legs. She was cutting the stem of a flower with her fingernail to thread a chain. In her hair she already wore a coronet of daisies that she had massacred some time before.

Bong! Bong! Bong! Six o'clock.

'Annice! Are you up there?'

I think now that that was my first visit to Caffelmeade, though at the time I told myself that I had fallen asleep. But even then I knew, deep down, that it was like no dream that I had ever had. For a start I knew who they were, even knew their names. The woman was Elizabeth Wolsington, her daughters were Flora and Rosie, the boy was David Bennett, and the man was his uncle, Matt Bennett. I even knew the name of the cat. She was called Grisaille. I might have made up the names because I often wove stories in my head to entertain myself, but then, I also knew that the maze was made of privet, *Ligustrum ovalifolium*. Now how could I know that?

'Annice! Answer me please!'

I rolled reluctantly on to my front and shouted down the stairwell, 'Yes. I'm here!'

'What are you doing?' my mother called back.

I hastily picked up a book.

'Just reading!'

4

*Nothing could be more unnatural than a rose
garden. It has taken more than four thousand years
of gardening to produce the modern rose. The damask
rose* (Rosa damascena) *seen on frescoes from the
sixteenth century* BC *was already a hybrid of* Rosa
gallica *and* Rosa phoenicia. *A collection of
floribundas, climbers, miniatures, ramblers, and tea
roses found in any cottage garden is the manifestation
of a dream, the culmination of human will.*

I got off the bus and swung my almost empty bag on
to my shoulders. The new school was old. I had
arrived early having misjudged the distance and the
buses. I did not want to stand idly with nothing to do, so I
started to walk round the perimeter. What at first I took
to be the main building was in fact just the oldest. It
looked more like a town hall than a place for children.
Behind it was a squat block of shabby classrooms,
temporary accommodation for the raising of the school
leaving age. Temporary, nearly thirty years ago. Then there
was the glass and steel five-storey tower that I had thought
was behind the school but could now see was part of it.
If there had ever been an original ground-plan it had long
disappeared beneath a scattering of huts which had been
put higgledy-piggledy on every available bit of land,
looking like fungal growths. The tall black railings with
spear-shaped tops designed to keep both out and in, went
right round the compound. It was damp and cold, the sort

of creeping chill that makes the bones ache and the skin itch.

Caffelmeade in the summer! I could smell it.

I looked up to the top floor of the new building and saw that a woman, gripping a steaming cup, was looking out of the headteacher's conning tower apparently directly at me. I winced. Another new person, another person to get to know; but before we could know each other there would be mistakes, there would be misunderstandings, there would be strife. This was my experience.

Children were now arriving at a run with schoolbags jumping on their backs, or dawdling with schoolbags trailing, or skidding bicycles to a halt, or tumbling from cars, or squeezing out of the doors of buses. There was the usual mêlée of small fry in, this time, royal blue jumpers or blazers, and amongst them the older boys with an inch of leg between their trousers and socks or with trousers sweeping the ground, and the older girls with skirts hitched to a fashionable length. I watched as these older ones formed into clumps. My mother had advised me once that I should watch for any lone person who seemed about the same age and should attach myself to them until I found my bearings. I knew from experience that this was not a good thing. People who walk alone in year eleven do so for good reason. I held my head up, set my face to impassive and went in.

The inside was even more depressing than the outside. Every school has its own smell compounded of chalk dust, lab chemicals, and bodies. This one also had the sweet stench of bad drains and heavily perfumed disinfectant. The original building, where the school office was, had green glazed tiles to waist height, many of them chipped and most of them worn dull. Above that the walls were painted in the kind of pale brown that you always get when you mix odds and ends of colours, and whatever posters had been there had been ripped away leaving the remains of Sellotape and Blu-Tack and pock-marked plaster. Dry rot spread from the corners and down from the ceilings. A teacher was busy attaching lining paper to cover the worst of the damage. It was cold.

The day was much like a first day anywhere else. I was seen by the headteacher, a brisk, smart, business woman who told me how unfortunate it was having to change schools so close to my GCSE examinations but assured me that it was a friendly school and all would be well. I was seen by my form tutor, a middle-aged, long-haired, track-suited man who told me how unfortunate it was having to change schools so close to my GCSE examinations but assured me that it need not upset me if I put enough energy into it. I was talked to by a number of girls in my form and looked over by a number of the boys. They all said how hard it must be for me changing schools so close to my GCSE examinations but assured me that I would soon fit in. I was surprised that the idea of changing school near Christmas in year eleven should be met with such unanimous dismay. At my last school the examinations were something that everyone knew would happen but which did not figure very largely in their thoughts. I felt that my parents were being held to blame for what was seen in this school as an incredible misfortune. Of course I blamed my parents constantly, but I did not like others blaming them without even knowing them.

'It's my father's work,' I explained. 'He's in the theatre.'

I knew, of course, that this gave the wrong impression. I could tell by the looks of envy and mock disbelief that they thought he was an actor or a director. I did not want to tell them that he was in administration and that he dealt with 'front of house' because they would think that this meant just selling tickets.

I was standing at the bus stop at the end of the day waiting for a bus into the city centre, when a girl with short butter-coloured hair came to stand by me.

'Hello,' the girl said. 'Do you live in town too?'

'No,' I told her, 'I get another bus from town. I live right out in the country.'

It was as though someone else had said this. I had not meant to lie. I had no reason to lie. It was said without any thought at all.

'Oh!' the girl murmured. 'That must be nice.'

I said nothing more. The girl continued herself, 'I suppose you have a big garden then?'

'Yes. We have a big garden.'

'We don't, just a patio. Well, a yard really, but it's very nice.'

I smiled politely.

'I'm Heather,' the girl said.

'Annice.'

'I thought that you might live near the theatre.'

'No.'

Another lie. I was now on automatic pilot.

'It must be lovely. You must know loads of famous people.'

'Some,' I answered truthfully.

'I thought that you were artistic as soon as I saw you.'

'Why?'

'You know. The way you look. Your clothes. Your hair. Everything.'

'I haven't got uniform because there's really not much point for so short a time. Apart from that I look the same as everyone else, don't I?'

Heather rolled her eyes and laughed.

26

'Do you have any brothers or sisters? I'm an only one.'

'I have a little sister,' I heard myself say, 'Rosie. She's five.'

When we got to the bus station Heather turned towards my house, and to keep up the pretence of the house in the country I had to set off in the other direction towards the country buses. I looked over my shoulder to see if I could go back but Heather was still watching me. We waved. Heather stood her ground. I had no option but to walk away in the wrong direction.

I made the best of it by going to the art gallery. I could spend an hour there before anyone would miss me at home. This time I made no pretence of looking at other pictures but went straight to the end room. I took off my multicoloured duffel coat and sat against the radiator rubbing my hands. I was warm for the first time that day.

I looked at my coat. My mother had made it from an old white blanket, dying the pieces scarlet and mustard and purple. She had cut them into jigsaw shapes and then sewn them together into a jacket with a hood and toggle fasteners. I think that my mother was happiest doing things with her hands. She ought to have lived in a country cottage and made jam and patchwork bedspreads instead of getting into suits and pounding a typewriter. I loved my jigsaw coat, but now I saw it through Heather's eyes and my pleasure was spoiled, for I did not want to be different.

I went to stand in front of the pictures. In the photograph I could see the path down which I had walked in the dream and if I went really close I fancied that I could see the centre of the maze where the Wolsingtons had been sitting. I turned through what looked like a rose-covered trellis. There were twenty or so people gathered on a small lawn.

I saw them straight away.

Elizabeth was walking towards the middle of the lawn where a glazed dragon shot fountains of water from its nostrils, splashing the dust away from its scales to disclose veridian green, cobalt blue, and the remains of gold. The dragon fountain was set on a stone pedestal inside a smooth basin. I watched her reach down amongst the water-lilies and bring out a bottle. Carelessly, she wiped her hand down the folds of her cream skirt. Such disregard for both the oriental dragon and her dress shocked and charmed me at the same time.

'Now, what would you like to do?' Elizabeth asked.

I thought for a moment that she was talking to me.

'Don't know,' Rosie answered. She was not wearing the kimono from the painting, but her dress was the same intense pink.

'Then let's walk around and I'll tell you about the roses.'

She took the little girl's hand and they set off.

'This hedge is made up of two old bush roses. This one is *Rosa alba*, the mother of them all. It's the White Rose of York. The other one is the Red Rose of Lancaster.'

Rosie looked at the fully open dishes of dark purplish pink.

'But it's not red.'

'No, it isn't.'

'Are they all old roses?' she asked. 'Are all our roses special?'

A rose, I thought, is a rose, is a rose.

'Some of them are quite rare, I believe, but you aren't really interested in the roses are you?' Elizabeth asked. 'Wouldn't you rather go and play?'

'Yes, I am,' Rosie answered quickly. She would rather go and play, of course. Of course she would. But she also wanted to be part of the grown-up party. I knew exactly what Rosie was thinking and I realized I also knew exactly what Elizabeth Wolsington was thinking. I knew their every nuance of thought and feeling. Strangely, I did not then wonder at this. 'What's that one?' Rosie asked.

She pointed to a rose that was deep pink in the bud, but which furled back to petals that were but faintly blushed.

'That looks more like a real rose.'

'That's "Wolsington's China Pink",' Elizabeth said.

She picked a leaf, crumpled it and then held out her palm.

'What does that remind you of?' she asked, holding it up to her daughter's face.

'It smells of tea, that funny green tea.'

'Yes. It's one of the first tea roses. At the end of the eighteenth century some ancestor or other created this from *Rosa chinensis* and *Rosa gigantica* and some unknown other species that he brought back from China.'

She broke one off and gave it to Rosie but the little girl did not hold it properly and it fell to the ground.

The scent of the roses was heavy, lulling, drugging. I could smell burning, the acrid sappy smell of a garden bonfire. Now I could see nothing but thick black smoke. My eyes watered and then prickled and turned red. My throat burned, swelled and then closed, cutting off the air supply. The fire smouldered with dirty heat and I would almost have welcomed a flame for its cleanness.

It seemed a long time before it cleared and then I saw that little remained of the rose garden. The blackened ground was steaming and smoke rose in little puffs as Matt turned the charcoaled remains of the roses with his boots. The leather was peeling and the sole gaped. He was wearing the sweatshirt that he had on in the painting, but his hair was only grey with ash. He thrust his hands under his arms, hugging himself. The scaly dragon was grooved with soot, its glaze dulled and blistered.

'Just one careless cigarette,' Elizabeth said.

'Not a cigarette,' Matt said bluntly.

'I know that they were important plants, but we should be glad that no one was hurt,' Elizabeth soothed.

'It's not the plants,' he replied. 'I have cuttings from the very old ones. They'll grow again. What really hurts is the spite.'

'You can't call an accident spiteful.'

'That you can't.'

'But it was an accident! The firefighters said spontaneous combustion.'

'Aye. Just the right plants come together to produce just the right gases that burst into flames by themselves.'

'It sounds so unlikely when you put it like that,' she said.

'Unlikely or not,' Matt said grimly, 'the garden has done this to itself.'

'Mummy!'

Flora was at the top of a long series of stone steps. She was wearing a yellow dress of some thin fabric and a large floppy hat and, even in her distress, she looked strong and healthy and shining as though she carried her own source of sunlight with her.

'Oh! Isn't it awful?' she cried and began to run down towards us.

'Careful!' Matt called. 'The steps are slippery.'

The steps may well have been slippery but it was the hosepipe that caught her; not the white firefighters' hose as thick as a man's arm, but the thin green snake used to water the garden. She fell heavily and awkwardly and she did not get up. It has taken me longer to remember this than it took to happen. Flora called from the top of the steps, as golden and sturdily slim as a daffodil and then she was lying broken at the bottom.

I looked down and saw the rose that her mother had dropped. It lay, strangely perfect, on the blackened earth. This might be the very last Wolsington China Pink. I picked it up. Its petals felt cool, almost like paper.

'They're not real,' a man's voice said, 'but they're very good. They fool a lot of people.'

I turned to see a gallery attendant. I held a silk rose in my hands. He gently took it from me and put it back in the vase.

I looked at the photograph again and then at the painting. Where the rose garden had been was painted over with thick black paint overlayered with ash grey.

'Do you know what kind of roses they are?' I asked.

'Pink,' he replied.

I just made it to the cloakroom before I was sick.

5

*Père David, a French Jesuit priest, travelled to China
and he brought home* Davida involucrata, *the
handkerchief tree, but it died. An expedition was sent
to China to get some seeds, and they ran into all
kinds of problems: imprisonment, fever, and rapids.
When, at last, they found the parent tree it was dead.
After many adventures, they stumbled across one in
full flower, but had to wait for the seeds to ripen. It
was the time of the Boxer Rebellion and they retreated
to Peking.*

N othing more happened for a few weeks. I did not
find myself in the garden at Caffelmeade again,
but then I did not go to the gallery either. I almost
forgot about it. Almost.

I did my best to settle in to school and apart from
the story about living in the country and having a little
sister I even managed to tell the truth. The trouble
started again because of an English lesson.

I had had some incompetent teachers, I had had some
uninspiring teachers, I had had some boring teachers but I
had never had a teacher yet more consistently
incompetent, uninspiring, and boring as Mr Watson, my
new English teacher.

'This is not a play for children,' Mr Watson said to
the English class uncertainly as though reading from an
instruction book. 'It's not about fairies.' He waited for
the inevitable snigger and then continued, 'Forget the

gauzy sprites swinging over the stage on wires, forget the whimsy.' He gave every word equal ponderous weight, as though he was driving a juggernaut down the slow lane of a very straight motorway. This had the effect of lulling us to sleep. It was his way of getting through his lesson, through his day, through his life.

He was a tall man, entirely straight lines and acute angles, as though drawn with a ruler and set-square. He looked around and sighed and cracked his knuckles. Some of the class were staring out of the window at the patch of sky which represented longed-for freedom, some were quietly getting on with other things, maths homework, shopping lists, love letters. A few, a happy few, were actually listening to him.

They, he must have realized sadly, were mostly the ones who were going to be in the play. There was Elspeth who, with the removal of a mere elastic band could change from stately Hippolyta to wanton Titania; there was Barry who was to be Theseus and Oberon, not because he could act well but because he was the only boy in the class taller than Elspeth; there were Philip and Sam, brothers, ready made for Lysander and Demetrius. After this the casting of Heather as Helena was automatic as she and Sam had been glued together since the second year.

The rude mechanicals had been easy enough to find. There were enough comics in the class. He had not yet found Puck but, he told us, he was not worried by this as there was a talented child in Year Seven who could do it at a pinch. It was Hermia that bothered him. He had yet to find anyone who could say the verse and who looked right.

'The headmistress,' he almost shouted, startling the class into attention, 'has deemed it right that we should put on this play after the exams and what our headmistress deems to be right, lo! is right. She exhorts us to remember

33

that our exam text was not meant to be read but to be performed. Miss Ogle is directing the play. She leads and lo! we follow.'

The class was settling back, having decided that it was only Mr Watson warbling rubbish as usual, when he shouted, 'You, girl. What's your name?'

'Annice Campbell.'

'Have I seen you before?'

'Yes, but I've only been here a few weeks.'

'Stand up.'

I had a book open on my lap. I could probably have fumbled it on to my seat but something in the way he had snapped 'Stand up' made me get up slowly and put the book down openly on my desk.

'What are you reading?'

'It's a collection of critical essays on *A Midsummer Night's Dream*,' I said.

Mr Watson snorted in disbelief and walked up to me. He picked up the book and then said, 'Yes, well, why are you reading it now?'

The class fell silent.

'It's the English lesson,' I replied reasonably enough.

'But you should be listening to me,' he stated, 'not reading. Anyway, I've never heard of this book.'

'Oh! It's good. Would you like to borrow it?'

The class drew in its breath.

'You're about five feet tall?' Mr Watson asked.

I began to wonder if the man was actually unhinged.

'About that, yes.'

'You'll do,' he said decisively.

'Do what?'

'You're Hermia,' he said just as the bell went.

Heather joined me at the bus stop. It was already becoming routine.

'What about Mr Watson?' she asked. 'A collection of critical essays! What about his face when he saw that it really was that?'

I smiled.

'Would you like to borrow it?' Heather quoted and laughed.

'It wasn't supposed to be funny,' I said. 'I just thought that he might get a better idea of the play if he read them.'

Heather regarded me shrewdly for a while and then said, 'I bet you did at that.'

'Well, he's not very good, is he?'

'He's awful.'

'How will you all get through the exam?'

'Oh, Miss Ogle is quite different. Now that you're Hermia you'll see. I'm Helena.'

'Who's Demetrius?'

Heather flushed very slightly.

'Sam.'

'He's the one with the shoulders who looks like a quarterback.'

'He's big, yes,' Heather said huffily.

'He's your boyfriend?'

Heather nodded.

'Who's Lysander?' I asked.

'Phil, Sam's brother.'

'They don't look like brothers, except for size.'

'Phil's adopted. They've been brought up more or less as twins but he's a headcase. He's bright, and I mean bright! His brain would light up Wembley Stadium.'

I smiled and Heather added, 'But he's a bit weird. He reads a lot. He reads Dawkins, and Hawking, and Eco. Ever heard of them?'

I nodded.

'Have you? Oh! Well he also reads Asimov and Adams. *The Hitchhiker's Guide to the Galaxy*? You know?'

I nodded again.

'He thinks that he's scientific, but you never know where science ends and science fiction begins with Philip. I'm not sure that he knows himself.'

'We are talking about the boy with the hair and . . . and everything?' I asked.

'I know!' Heather sighed. 'He's drop-dead-gorgeous as well! He should be pale and skinny and spotty, shouldn't he? There's no justice in the world.'

'And he can act?'

'Well . . .'

'He's no good?'

'He was in a pantomime once and, well, it's all right till he speaks.'

'What's wrong?'

'I'm not sure. I think it's his voice.'

'The accent?'

'Not so's you'd notice,' Heather said a bit huffily. 'It's more like dreary, boring, like a mechanical robot.'

Heather said no more about Phil as the bus rumbled the few yards between each stop. I had noticed him, of course. Along with every other girl in the school, I had noticed him. Now, I wondered how I was going to get along with a boy who looked like Young Lochinvar but sounded like a depressed robot.

'Perhaps your dad could help with the play?' Heather asked as the bus trundled into the city centre.

'He's very busy,' I said quickly.

'My mother's doing the costumes. She works as a machinist so it's no trouble for her. What does your mother do?'

'Nothing. I mean she works in the house and the garden and she does committees and things.'

'She doesn't have a proper job?'

I could have left it there, but before I could stop myself I had added, 'Well, it's a big house and it's a very old garden. She's writing a book about plants.'

'A gardening book?'

'More about where the plants come from originally.'

'Oh!' Heather said.

'She's an amateur naturalist,' I added.

'Ah!' Heather said.

After this I walked straight to the gallery. I had to. I got a beaker of water from the café and took it with me to the end room. The attendant followed me in.

'Food and drink not allowed.'

'It's only water.'

'Just a minute,' he said and was gone. He came back in a little while with a folding canvas stool that had an easel attached. He placed it before the pictures.

'Look, you can put your water in the holder there as if you were going to paint.'

'Water's allowed for painting but not for drinking?'

'That's it.'

I sat down gingerly but the contraption was more stable than I had thought.

'Are you doing a project?' he asked.

'Maybe,' I smiled at him. 'I'm thinking of it.'

He smiled back and left me. I looked at the pictures and particularly at Elizabeth Wolsington.

'Why are you doing this to me?' I asked her. 'Whenever someone asks me about my mother I think of you.'

The woman looked impassively out from the frame unaware of me or my questions. I looked into the distance in the painting. There, amongst the surrounding meadows was a tiny building with a wooden scaffold for a swinging sign. The sign had gone. I looked at the photograph and found the building. The sign was in place. On it was a crude representation of flowers and a man in black. I had to crane my neck to read the sign, but was not surprised to see, when I got close enough, that it said 'The Amateur Naturalist'.

The room collapsed into whiteness. It would be just as sensible to say that the room expanded into whiteness. I felt that it did both of these things. Once again I felt centred and at the same time dispersed. I know that I am describing it badly. Perhaps that is because we do not have the words that I need, words that say both nowhere and everywhere at the same time, both nothing and everything. How could we?

Then I was surrounded by poppies, not the gallant scarlet weed of the cornfield but overblown carmine red orientals, their necks drooping, laying their heavy heads at unlikely angles. There were many different poppies, strange pinks like blood in water, Himalayan icy frozen blues, Welsh as lemon green as the edge of a bruise, bitter sweet poppies, vibrant with colour and steeped in death.

Flora was sitting in a chair with piles of papers on her lap which, from time to time, she read, but mostly she turned them over with little more than a glance. David was working near her, filling stone urns and terracotta pots with almost fully grown geraniums. Strawberries had felt their way through the loose stones during the hot months and now they were drying out, but next year their leaves would make a carpet reclaiming the path.

'Listen to this, Matt,' she called.

He did not acknowledge her but I knew that he was somewhere in the herbaceous border. Sometimes as Flora read to him he knelt and rocked rhythmically, his hands tearing at the intruding plants. He turned himself into a weeding machine, switching himself on physically, needing only a very small part of his brain. His mind was free to wander, or to listen to her.

As before, I knew all this at some level deeper than conscious thought. I knew this as surely as I knew anything. I knew, not just what they said, but what they thought and what they felt. I did not wonder at this. It felt right.

'Listen to this, Matt,' Flora said again, not deterred by his lack of response. 'This is a letter from someone called Richard. It's from China. He says, *"So you see, my dear, why I really must stay, don't you? After so many disappointments, just when we had given up looking for Père David's tree, we have found it. We have come across a clump of them, but they are in full flower and we shall not be able to collect ripe seeds for a few weeks. You must not be too worried. We are quite safe, as safe as if we were in Peking."'*

Matt continued to weed as though he had heard nothing.

'He must have been an ancestor,' she suggested.

'He was your great-grandfather,' Matt informed her without breaking his rhythm. 'He was Richard Wolsington.'

'How do you know?'

'I've heard of him,' was all he said in a tone that closed the subject.

'Will you tell me about Richard Wolsington, Matt?' Flora wheedled in mockery of her childhood lisp. 'Tell me about my great-grandfather.'

'There was a French Jesuit priest called Père David, who travelled to China and brought some specimen trees back to Europe,' Matt replied and then told her of the troubled quest for the handkerchief tree. 'And then someone climbed out on a four inch branch, two hundred feet above the ground, and took some seeds and a photograph. The first handkerchief tree flowered in England in 1911.'

'So my great-grandfather brought some seeds home?' she said when he had finished.

Matt smiled a queer smile.

'Not quite. Your great-grandmother persuaded him to retreat to Peking to be safe and he died during the siege.'

'How sad! Then we didn't get the seeds?'

'David'll show you,' Matt said.

'Right now?' David asked.

Matt nodded. David walked to Flora and took hold of the back of her chair. It was only then that I saw that she was in a wheelchair. I found that I was following. They went to the end of the long gravel path to where a seat had been placed against the wall, then turned on to a narrower rough path that led through the beeches. It was cooler under the dark canopy, but when I looked up the sun burnished the edges of the leaves, kindling fire, and I felt hot again. I was running, not smoothly, but in leaps as my feet alternately bumped over exposed roots and sank into the dry remains of last year's leaves. There was no undergrowth to slow me down. The earth had been denatured by the copper beeches.

Flora was angry.

'Don't go so fast, David,' she called to him. 'I'll fall out!'

David slackened his pace slightly but the chair still shook and rattled its way down through the wood, leaping and lurching.

'David!' Flora shouted, but I knew then that she was actually enjoying the ride, was excited by the apparent danger.

He stopped and then knelt down in front of her, flushed and breathing hard. He removed a leaf from her hair. His hand was cold against her cheek.

'That's better,' he said. 'You've got some colour in your cheeks. Why are you such a brat to Uncle Matt?'

Flora smiled. 'I'm fond of him. He understands.'

He stepped aside and waved his arm towards a tree.

'Oh!' she said. 'I see! You mean that's it?'

'That's *Davida involucrata*.'

The tree was in full summer glory, the white handkerchiefs of its flower bracts fluttering.

'I've always called it the dove tree,' she said. 'I should like to paint it some day.'

'It's also called a handkerchief tree and also a ghost tree,' he told her. 'Your great-grandmother had it planted. She gave my grandfather the seeds and he grew it there.'

'So it's our tree, yours and mine,' Flora said.

'You could say that of most of this garden. We've been here as long as you, though in a more humble capacity, of course.'

As he said this David tugged his forelock and Flora laughed.

'True. One forgets that one is consorting with a serf.'

I looked up into the branches and a rogue breeze made them wave back cheerily from a clear China-blue sky. Slowly the sky darkened until it was like midnight-blue velvet and then the moon came from behind a stray cloud and I saw that I was at the top of the gravel path just outside the house. The moon was bright, the patches of poppies held blue lagoons in their fully blown heads, the birch was outlined with silver.

I walked down the wide gravel path, swiftly and lightly so that the sharp stones would not hurt my feet. When I reached the wall at the end I realized that the seat was not there. There was a small basin set to catch water as it trickled from a lion's mouth set halfway up the wall. I heard footsteps and slipped into the path

41

that David had taken, but there was no path, no pressed dirt track through the copper beeches, in fact no copper beeches. The trees above my head were elms, ancient elms with bifurcated trunks and deeply scarred bark. The undergrowth was soft and wet beneath my feet.

I could see the fountain and the woman who had come to it. The woman wore a long white nightdress and a silk shawl. The colours of the shawl showed softly, Paisley curls of blue and green and purple, the silver and gold threads glistening as she moved. She held a letter in her hand and a crumpled envelope. She sank down by the basin and began to cry, silently at first and then with deep ugly sobs. I tried to move towards her but although I walked I got no closer. After a while the woman scrubbed at her face with the shawl and opened the envelope. On to her hands fell seeds. She clasped these very tightly and ran away. The back of the shawl was black where it had trailed in the water.

The thunder rolled and I could hear the rain and see the leaves starting to bend under the weight. I found that when I walked now I moved forward and once out on the gravel path, I felt the rain. As she ran back towards the house the lightning began to fork, splitting the sky into crazy paving. Then there was nobody on the path before me. The thunder rolled again and far away at the bottom of the path there was no longer a fountain, there was the dove tree and it was spitting fire as the lightning clove it apart.

I opened my eyes to find that I had tipped the glass of water over, soaking my dress in patches. I jumped up and, holding the glass in both shaking hands, stood before the painting. The tree was gone. The painter had driven a great wedge of daylight down the trunk chiselling it apart like kindling, the charred branches stark against the sky. One great bough had been severed. It lay, bent unnaturally, like a broken arm. Its white handkerchiefs still waved in the breeze.

Then I ran.

6

*In 1826 a magnificent lily with raised carmine spots
was brought to Europe.*

The days passed quickly now. I was getting to know
people and starting to fit in. I was Annice, or even
Annie, now and not 'the new girl'. I did not go to
the gallery again although it would not be true to say that I
had quite forgotten about it because at the back of my
mind, even when I was talking to my new friends, even
when I was in class, there was always present a vague
foreboding, a feeling of menace that I associated with the
garden at Caffelmeade.

I had renewed *Naturalists both Amateur and Mercenary*
at the library and carried it with me. It was a book that
I could only read in short doses but I felt compelled to
finish it. It was as though tendrils were growing in my
mind, wrapping themselves gently but firmly around me.
Otherwise I was settling down well, almost content, until
that is, the first reading for *A Midsummer Night's Dream*.

> 'If thou love'st me, then
> Steal forth thy father's house tomorrow night;
> And in a wood a league without the town,
> Where I did meet thee once with Helena,
> To do observance to a morn of May,
> There will I stay for thee.'

'Hold it!'
Miss Ogle fetched a deep breath and then said, 'Philip,

you're not ordering a Big Mac. You want your girlfriend to leave her family and run off with you, not just for the evening, but for ever. Let's try once more.'

Philip went mechanically through the lines again.

If Mr Watson was drawn with a ruler then a compass was needed for Miss Ogle. Her body, with no defined waist, was a large circle, on top of which the smaller circle of her head was set like a cottage loaf, and then on top of that sat her tight bun like a currant. She had dimples even when not smiling, as though the dough of her cheeks had been pinched for decorative effect. Her tiny nose, unformed like a baby's, was not long enough to hold up her large square glasses, which slipped forward and which she constantly adjusted with the heel of her hand. Pushing escaped hair into the bun, flicking her glasses, tweaking her skirt down, pushing her sleeves up, Miss Ogle was a bustling mountain of fidget.

As she spoke she was sitting on a chair in the main body of the hall but some teachers have an amazing turn of speed and before I knew what was happening, she had rolled on to the stage, shouldered Philip away and was facing me with the book in her hand. She read the speech herself.

'Would you have gone with me?' she asked.

'I think I might,' I laughed.

'Do you hear that?' Miss Ogle thundered. 'She might have said yes to me! You have to admit that you've got the advantage there! Make her see it! Make her want to go with you! Can you do it?'

'I think I can,' Philip replied, 'but this is just a reading.'

'Tone, boy! Tone!' Miss Ogle screamed. She turned to the others.

'Elspeth, say "I'm just reading" as though your mother has accused you of doing something wrong.'

'I'm just *reading*!' Elspeth pleaded.

'Now you, Heather. Say it as though you have come across your little sister with her head in a book and you want her to put it down and do something more useful.'

'You're *just* reading,' Heather accused.

'Now you, Sam. Say it as though it's of no importance to you. Show that you're willing to stop immediately.'

'I'm just reading,' Sam said keeping the emphasis even, a slight inflection at the end.

'Annice. You say it as though everyone has been given something more important to do. Be resentful. Question.'

'*I'm* just reading?' I protested.

'There,' Miss Ogle said triumphantly, 'can you hear the difference, Philip?'

He nodded.

'Away we go again then.'

Once more he read the lines. This time he was animated but the emphasis kept falling on all the wrong syllables. However, Miss Ogle sighed and let us continue.

We were sitting in a circle on the stage. I sat next to Heather who read Helena with ease and wit using the same everyday tone she used for chatting on the bus. It worked well. Sam was a gullible but decent Demetrius and I started to think that despite his weight he might have made a better Lysander. Philip! I was even beginning to think that anyone would have been a better Lysander. He tossed back his long thick blond hair, revealed a classically handsome face that could have earned him a place on any catwalk, smiled his perfect smile and then spoke without any apparent understanding of the words.

'What, should I hurt her, strike her, kill her dead?
Although I hate her I'll not harm her so!'

—he intoned as though running through a shopping list.

The comic parts were read in such a way that any chance of laughter was squashed. The readers seemed to be perversely mistiming everything so that the jokes were killed. Miss Ogle halted them.

'You have read this play, I take it?' she asked.

No answer.

'Mr Watson has been teaching it for nearly two years, so I can assume that you at least know the story, can't I?'

No answer.

She looked at Heather who smiled lamely.

'Heather, you do know the play by now, don't you?'

Heather was embarrassed and did not know how to answer. I knew her problem. She could tell Miss Ogle that Mr Watson was hopeless but she knew that the class had colluded with him, taking the opportunity to be lazy. I had seen this often enough in all my schools. She was in a bind. She shrugged her shoulders.

'Well,' Miss Ogle said, 'we'll read through to the end and then we'll see. If you please, Hermia.'

The play ground on and finally came to an end. Miss Ogle gathered her things together.

'I'll take the ''mechanicals'' only tomorrow. We need to make this funny, give the audience a few clues that laughter would be appreciated. Lysander, you sound as though you have only known Hermia a few weeks.'

'I have,' Philip replied.

'No. You—Philip—have only known Annice for a few weeks and it shows. Lysander has known Hermia long enough to fall in love.'

Philip looked blankly beautiful. It was difficult to believe that he had one of the best brains in the school.

'Maybe you should get to know Annice a bit,' Miss

Ogle suggested. 'Talk to each other. We'll try the "lovers" again on Friday. In the meantime I want all of you to outline the plot and show how you see your own character on one side of A4 please.'

Heather looked to Sam and he held eight fingers up. They laughed.

'Is it funny, Sam? Is it funny, Heather?' Miss Ogle asked.

'No, Miss Ogle.'

There was the shuffle of bags as the group broke up and Sam and Heather were still laughing.

'What's the joke?' Philip asked.

'Sam is collecting things that people ask you to do on one side of A4,' Heather explained. 'You know, menus for *Masterchef*, what you would do if you were Prime Minister, your CV. You know the kind of thing. It's amazing what people think you can do on one side of A4.'

'What's the best so far?'

'Probably *Blue Peter*,' Sam replied. 'Suggestions on how to save the planet. With illustrations.'

They laughed.

'I'm waiting,' Sam continued, 'to be asked to say on one side of A4 what the best use is for one side of A4.'

'Philip, we're walking to the bus. Why don't you come with us?' Heather suggested. 'You've to get to know each other. Orders.'

There was a pause while Philip looked at me, a swift glance only but an assessment nevertheless, before he replied, 'I have homework to do.'

Heather gave me a little push towards him.

'Oh, come on,' Heather persisted. 'This is homework.'

'Sorry,' Philip muttered shrugging his bag on to his shoulder. 'Coming, Sam?'

Sam signalled resignation to Heather and followed his brother out of the hall.

I was hot. I felt the flush creep up my neck and hoped that the high black polo sweater hid most of it. I was both hurt and angry.

'Don't mind him,' Heather said kindly. 'He's always like that. It's just his way.'

'What does that mean?' I snapped. 'Of course it's "his way" and he's responsible for it!' Then I turned on Heather, 'And I'm not anyone's homework!' As I said it, I knew that I had set my own trap. I was less than his homework. He had said so.

I almost ran to the gallery.

I found myself beneath an apple tree. This time Caffelmeade had not taken me over. This time I had stood before the pictures and willed myself into them, had waited for the white light that preceded my transference. It had worked. I was at Caffelmeade.

Flora sat in the kitchen garden with a tray across her knees. She was sorting letters, some of them very old. David was lifting potatoes, turning up each plant, removing the tubers, carefully rubbing the black earth from them, and then putting them into boxes according to size. The leaves and roots were thrown on to piles at each end of the furrows. The grey cat slinked past me and sashayed towards Flora. Flora scooped it up and began to stroke it so that she could watch David without being seen to do so. She fingered his shirt, hanging over the back of her chair, and tears threatened. He looked up at her.

'What is it?'

'The sun's in my eyes,' she said lamely.

'Then put your sunglasses on, idiot,' he grinned.

'Why do you lift potatoes like that?'

49

'Like what?'

'Well, in just that way. Why do you clean them, why do you sort them into those boxes, why do you stack the waste in exactly the same place each year?'

'It's not exactly the same place. Last year the potatoes were over there. Crop rotation, you've heard of crop rotation?' he teased her.

It was a private joke yet I did not feel excluded.

'Yes, but I've watched Matt and I've watched you in the garden and it really could be the same person. I mean it could be either of you, you do things in the same way.'

'It's a way that has the seal of time. My uncle taught me and his father taught him, and maybe we vary it slightly. I mean, he's taller than me and so the waste pile is probably that bit further away, but there's no point in re-inventing the wheel.'

'It's comforting.'

He looked at her and they both smiled slowly.

A lump rose in my throat and I felt sad for myself. If only I was Flora. I had read so many books about family, about friendship, about love but I had never managed to find it in real life. I had never ever found easy companionship, not even as a small child. I had never found a way into the golden world of *Swallows and Amazons*. I was a cat who walked alone.

'There must have been a field of lilies somewhere this side of the wall once,' Flora said. 'There's a letter here about it from someone called William. It's dated 1827.'

'That's right,' David replied. 'It was just about here. You can see it on the engraving in the dining room.'

As he said this he heaved over a potato crown and then bent over and picked up a bulb.

'And every now and then, one comes up.'

I saw now that a small pile of bulbs sat on a sheet of newspaper.

'What do you do with them?'

'We plant them in the back of the herbaceous border.'

'Do they flower?'

'Some do.'

'Can you tell what they are?'

'I can't, but Matt often gets it right. It's a surprise present from the past.'

'How long can they lie dormant?'

'I don't know, but a long time. Archaeologists found some grain which had been spilled in a prehistoric settlement somewhere in Scotland. They planted and watered it and it grew.'

'So there could be anything lurking underneath the garden just waiting for the right conditions to come to the surface?'

'Well, not quite anything.'

'But lots of things that we don't know are there. The garden can wait patiently.'

'You talk as though it's a person, Flora! Gardens don't wait patiently, they don't wait at all, they don't have a will. They just are.'

'I sometimes feel that this garden is more than that. It's a living thing and we can nurture it, or neglect it, and in turn it either rewards us or sulks. Is that a bit fanciful?'

'It is, but you're an artist and so allowed to be a bit fey! This potato plant is alive, and those carrots, but the garden itself is neither alive nor dead. The garden is only an area of land that we choose to define. It's only an idea really.'

'Davy,' a child's voice called, 'have you seen Matt?'

I looked towards the gate and saw the crescent of white that meant that Rosie was hanging upside down.

'That child will fall on her head one day,' Flora said, 'and I think that perhaps we should give in and put her in dungarees. Her knickers are always on show.'

'He's in the maze, Rosie,' David called back. 'Why do you want him?'

Rosie replied but her words were strangled by the folds of her skirt which were wrapped around her face.

'Come here, Rosie,' Flora called. 'We can't hear you.'

The little girl dropped off the gate and got to her feet. With a wriggle she righted her dress and with great care tugged down her skirt, then she ran to them, her face hot and red. David stuck the fork into the ground again and lifted another plant. A bundle of hair and dried stems came up with the potatoes. Hastily he kicked it to one side and, using his boot, covered it with soil. The grey cat appeared and began to circle it. David lifted the cat into his arms.

'Not now, Grisaille,' he whispered to her.

'Matt is trimming the maze,' Flora said to Rosie. 'Why do you want him? Will we do?'

'I don't think so, 'cos Mummy said to tell him that we'll be going in a few minutes.'

'Does Mummy want to see him before you go?'

'Don't know.'

'Well, perhaps you should go just inside the maze and call to him.'

Rosie began to skip away and David called after her, 'Remember, don't go right in and get lost.'

She turned and waved and was gone.

David put the cat back on its feet and began to feel for the potatoes. Once again Grisaille began to circle and to make little darting forays to the overturned soil.

'No, Grisaille, it's too late,' he said gently moving her away with his foot.

'What is it?' Flora asked.

'Fieldmice,' David replied. 'It's a fieldmouse's nest.'

'Oh! Why didn't you show it to Rosie? She would be enchanted. Let me see.'

'Better not.'

'Did you put the fork through it?'

'I don't think so, but they're all dead anyway.'

'How do you know?'

'I've seen it before. The mice give birth in the late spring and then we come along and earth up the potatoes without seeing them. Sometimes the nest gets filled or tipped up.'

'The babies get smothered?'

'Yes. Or strangled by the plants.'

'You'd think that the mice would know better.'

'It's always the end of the rows. We're so close to the meadow.'

'Let me see anyway.'

'No. That's not all.'

'What then?'

'The plant goes on growing. Sometimes the roots and the bones get fused together. The plant feeds on the mice.'

I don't want to know this, I thought, this is not how it should be.

'I thought that vegetables were free of blood. I'll never eat a potato again!' Flora declared.

'Yes, you will. There's no point in being squeamish about it. We put bonemeal and blood into the soil to enrich it remember, but of course it comes in nice clean boxes and doesn't look much like baby mice, so I suppose that makes it all right.'

'A garden is not always a lovesome thing.'

'No.'

'Matt,' Rosie called, peering round the first turning

53

in the maze. The hedgecutters went on humming. She turned the first corner and called again. Still no reply.

'Right, then left, then left,' she chanted as she went deeper in.

I was following her. The path here was overgrown, the hedges bellying inwards. I turned a corner and a man and woman came towards me. He was almost running, pulling her behind him, eager. She was laughing.

She was wearing a white muslin dress with tiny sleeves, a low frilled neck, and a black velvet ribbon tied under her breasts. Her hair was piled high and tiny ringlets sprang around her forehead.

'There will be the lily of various colours, that's a magnificent whitish pink with blood red spots. It's warty,' he said.

'Warty? William.'

'Yes, sort of blistered. Then there will be the orange devil lilies, spotted purple and black, and the Japan lilies, they're pink opening to white and they have a wonderful perfume. We'll have a whole field of them.'

'The lilies of the field?'

'Yes.'

'Matt!' Rosie was crying now and running blindly. She had quite lost track of the turns and was blundering into cul-de-sacs.

'Stand still, Rosie,' Matt called, 'and I'll find you. There you are!'

The little girl hurled herself at him and he said, 'You are a silly goose, Rosie.'

'Not!'

He tried to take hold of her but Rosie was a flailing bundle of shame and anger.

'Not a silly goose!'

'Of course you aren't! It's just words. Remember,

"Sticks and stones can break my bones, but words will never hurt me." '

That's not true. Bones mend.

'I have homework to do.'

I had steamed up the gallery window and I leaned my forehead against the damp glass. I was hot. Words, I thought, I'm full of words. I've read so many words that they're making me sick.

7

1991 was celebrated as the tercentenary of the maze at Hampton Court, although a 'cradle work of hornbeam' a 'perplexed twining of trees' was already there in 1662.

I was wakened early the next Saturday and knew immediately that something had happened. I squinted at my illuminated clock. Six. I could hear none of the usual noises of the city waking, and no colours danced on the wall. I pulled the duvet more closely round me, looked up at the roof and realized that the skylight was totally black, not just the dark of a cloudy night, but truly black as though some big animal had settled across the glass.

The chair was cold to my bare feet. I undid the latch and pushed at the window frame half expecting it to be heavy, but it opened easily and wet snow slid from it. I looked out, but instead of the rooftops of Manchester I saw the Wolsington's rose garden, its fire damped down beneath a white fall of ash. This frightened me and I struggled to bring back the chimneys, but the garden was more vivid than reality. I scraped up a handful of snow and rubbed it on my face. I opened my eyes again. A pigeon had been walking on the roof leaving circles of arrow prints in the snow. I shivered.

Of course I knew what was real and what was not. Nevertheless, although my mother was working all day and my father would be shut in his workshop, I decided that it would be best to give the gallery a rest. I would go to a park and walk until it was time for the rehearsal.

The play was coming together except, that is, for Lysander. The longer I spent with Philip the more distant he became; the more we practised, the more stilted he was. I was beginning to wonder if one of us would have to give up their part.

'The chemistry's not right,' Heather had comforted me. 'It's nothing personal.'

'If my chemistry isn't personal I don't know what is,' I replied.

'Don't mind so much. Your dress is nearly done. Can you come for a fitting? Come for tea after the rehearsal on Saturday.'

I thought now of the dress and smiled. Heather's mother was trying to make the costumes from drawings that I had taken from my father's desk.

'They're a bit fanciful,' I had apologized as I showed them for the first time. 'Costume's not his thing really. They're just doodles. What he'd like to see in his setting.'

'They're beautiful,' Miss Ogle replied, sifting through the sheets and laying them on the floor of the school hall.

'They're too difficult,' I apologized, 'and they'd cost a lot.'

'They're not easy,' Heather's mother agreed, 'but if they work! Oh, if they work!'

'Will you try, Mrs Hindle?' Miss Ogle asked.

'I'd like to. Yes, I'd really like to.'

Hermia's dress was in layers of different lengths, from sky blue through corn yellow to grass green, the top layer embroidered like a spring meadow.

'How do you get in and out of it?' Mrs Hindle asked.

I shrugged. 'He's not much on practicality.'

'Well, I'll have to work out a way. I'll think of something, even if I have to sew you into them on the night.'

I dressed quickly in the chill of the attic. The fire would be set ready to light downstairs, but I could not get used to the cold of a house without central heating. I looked in the mirror at my pale, stiff face muffled up in sweater and scarves and imagined myself in the stage costume. I could see how I might look. I could also see Flora reflected, Flora in a floaty dress printed with wild flowers. I could see the back as she sat at the table. It was low and there was lacing that pulled the bodice closely to her waist. I shook my head and the mirror reflected back only my own pinched face.

I climbed on the chair to close the fanlight and took another look out. I shivered. The city sky was again heavy with snow, the translucent grey cut into by the black teeth of chimneys and roofs. I gulped in the early morning air which was surprisingly gentle now that the wind had stopped. My cheeks felt both warm and cold at the same time.

'There,' Flora said, 'I'll paint you there. In front of the white border.'

'Get out of my head!' I shouted and slammed the skylight shut.

I put on my mother's mukluks, bought for a ski trip that never happened. The snow had already turned to slush in the streets and I had to jump over filthy grey puddles collected around every drain, their surfaces a rainbow of oil slicks broken by lumps of unrecognizable litter. The only park that I knew was that surrounding the art gallery and for an hour I walked resolutely round its paths. Then I went out on to the untrodden lawn and began to make the pattern of a maze.

I had had the park to myself, but now I was aware of someone else, someone watching me. I spun round but could see nothing. There was no colour except for the sickening bruise of yellow beneath each snow-laden cloud.

'Hello,' I called.

No answer.

I started to move again, scraping my feet sideways to make little snow walls. I stopped. I started again, a bit quicker. I stopped. Whatever I did the other did too. I heard him behind me as I walked, but when I listened, silence. Then I ran. I ran without heeding my paths, squashing down the maze. A figure detached itself from the trees and stood in my way.

'What are you doing here so early?' I demanded, then, 'Why are you following me?'

'I'm not following you. I work here at weekends, in the kitchen,' Philip replied equally crossly.

'Oh! I didn't know that you worked here.'

'Why should you? You only ever go to that one room in the gallery. I've seen you. Are you going there now?'

'No, just walking.'

'You've made a maze.'

'Yes.'

'It's spoiled.'

'It doesn't matter.'

We walked together up the long drive towards the gallery which loomed dark in the cold mist. The silence between us was heavy and uncomfortable. I asked questions but only got curt replies, sometimes merely a grunt. Eventually I said desperately, 'I'm sorry you obviously don't like me much. It wouldn't matter, but for the play.'

'I don't "not like you",' he mumbled. 'We're just so different.'

'How?'

'I don't like make-believe. I'm interested in things that you can know for certain.'

'Like what?'

'Like this snow that I can feel, like the fact that we're in Manchester, things like that.'

'How do you know that the snow is real? How do you know that any of it is real?'

'Of course the snow is real. I can see it.'

'But can you be sure that Canada is real?'

'Of course.'

'How? Have you been there? Have you seen it?'

'No, but other people have.'

'And you trust them?'

'All right. Maybe I believe that Canada is there rather than know it.'

'What would you say if I told you that the garden in the painting in the gallery is real and that I can walk into it? Would you believe that?'

'I would say that I believe that the garden is real in the same way that Canada is real, because people I have no reason to distrust tell me so. It's a reasonable belief. Anyway, what do you mean, you can walk into it?'

'When I stand in front of it I can fancy that I am actually there, actually at Caffelmeade.'

'That's just what I mean. You have a vivid imagination. You're a dreamer. I'm interested in concrete things, hard facts.'

'Then you wouldn't say that I'm really able to walk into the garden at Caffelmeade? I'm not really there?'

'Oh, come on!'

'Then why does it seem so real? As real as the snow, as real as Manchester.'

I had not meant to go into the gallery and until I met Philip I was content not to. Now, however, standing on the steps in the cold February air the golden warmth of the lighted windows were too much to resist. I had frightened myself and was cold. I would just take a quick look, but first I would have a coffee.

I sat in the window of the café with the big bowl of milky coffee, looking out at the silver rimed oak tree. I fancied that, in spite of the snow, the buds were beginning to swell. My eyes kept swinging back to the counter and the door which led to the kitchen.

Bother it, I thought, I'm not as dreamy as he makes out! I can spend a whole day without once pretending anything. So saying to myself, I fetched a book out of my coat pocket. All my coats and bags had books in them that could be dipped into anytime, anywhere. I would as soon leave the house without clothes as without reading matter. My father's library book was still in the pocket.

I leafed through the pages casually but then, little by little, I began to read it. An engraving of a giant pitcher plant caught my eye, the more because a name in the text stood out as though printed in red. 'Esther Wolsington'.

'Esther Wolsington was the eldest daughter of a family who lived in Northumberland in the 1880s. She had no inclination for marriage but her younger sister had and in those days it was thought bad manners for the younger to marry first. Esther saw that she was a barrier to her sister's happiness and decided to remove herself. She volunteered for the mission field and was sent to Sarawak. She married her co-worker, a formal arrangement of no consequence to either of them. Anyway, her husband died promptly on arrival and Esther was left to her own devices. She stayed in Sarawak for six years. There were many plant collectors around that part of the world at that time and they all collected the giant pitcher plant, Nepenthes rajah, but none of them got

*it safely home. Esther did so eventually by hiding the plants in
her stays, making oilskin packets which she attached to the
whalebones in her corsets. This way they were kept both moist and
warm. This resourceful woman later married her husband's
nephew and they returned to Sarawak. This time it seems the
marriage was not just for propriety.'*

I got hotter and hotter, what with the coffee and the
layers of clothes I had put on. I looked out of the window
and could only see white mist. The mist seemed to be
moving in layers and the layers were getting thinner.
Through them I could see the darkest of living greens and
then flashes of intense colour.

'This way, Esther,' a voice called and the curtain
was lifted a little.

I saw a woman, upright in a heavy straight skirt
and closely fitting jacket, bend her head to pass through.
I hurried after her, feeling tough wet vegetation under
my inexplicably bare feet. The woman was forging ahead
with determination. She wore a hard brimmed hat tied
down with veiling, and on her feet her dainty buttoned
boots had turned green. She cleared the trailing fronds
with a rolled parasol.

'Here it is,' the voice said, and I could now see a
man. He was wearing a loose jacket and trousers in the
same dirty white as the woman's outfit. His sola topi
perched on thick red hair and sweat ran down from his
forehead, over his cheeks and into his clerical collar, in
a steady stream. 'Here it is.'

He was holding a jug in one hand and he reached
for the pitcher suspended from the plant. The giant
pitcher was green and cream, with veining the colour of
dried blood. He poured the water into the jug and then
poured it away. He did this six times.

'Six pints,' he said.

'There's a bigger one up there,' Esther pointed.

He stretched, jumped, and finally fell, bringing it down on top of him. The contents of the pitcher flowed over him and Esther screamed. He flinched and then rallied.

'It's only a dead rat,' he said, picking it up by the tail and throwing it away.

'Annie!'

The water from the pitcher was hot as it soaked through on to my thigh.

'Annie, I've brought a cloth,' Philip said. I saw that I had pulled the coffee bowl over spilling coffee over the table. It was dripping on to my legs.

'You need to hold these bowls with both hands,' Philip instructed, and then seeing perhaps that I looked truly upset added, 'You'd be surprised how many people drop them.'

I made no effort to move and would have got very wet had he not caught the flow with the dishcloth.

'We should go soon if we're to get to school for the rehearsal. Anyway, you've not sat all morning in front of that painting. At least, you've spent it in the real world.'

I smiled but I was still shaking inside.

8

We came upon a splendid specimen of Nepenthes
rajah *in which there was a drowned rat.*

'We shall walk through the whole play this
afternoon,' Miss Ogle announced. 'I'm not
going to stop you except to work out
movement.'

'No chance!' Heather muttered.

Miss Ogle placed a chair and table in what would be
the centre front of the audience and asked us to begin.

'Now, fair Hippolyta, our nuptial hour
Draws on apace . . .'

'Stop!'

Heather caught my eye and we giggled.

'Theseus, you are addressing your bride-to-be in front
of courtiers. What do you think they will make of it if
you shout at her from as far away as you can physically
get? Look, this is like the photocalls that happen when
famous or royal couples announce their engagement.
Whatever subsequently happens to their marriage, at this
point they usually stand together.'

Saying this, she grabbed Barry's sleeve and tugged
him towards Elspeth.

I suppose that Miss Ogle kept to her promise and
did only stop us to work out choreography but this
meant stopping us at almost every page. Those who did
not understand the play were getting more and more

confused as she tried to make them see what was needed and those who did know it were bored.

Four hours after starting Puck lisped,

> *'Give me your hands, if we be friends,*
> *And Robin shall restore amends.'*

'Puck, why are you hopping on one leg?'

'I'm a bird.'

'You're what?'

Puck, who was being played by the precocious Year Seven boy recommended by Mr Watson, looked smug. He had the habit of miming odd words from the text such as undulating his hand when saying 'river', drawing a circle in the air for 'sun', clutching his chest as though shot with an arrow when saying 'love', and most irritating of all chucking himself under the chin when saying 'child' or 'boy'. His greatest moment came with

> *'Now the hungry lion roars*
> *And the wolf behowls the moon'*

when he rubbed his tummy on 'hungry', yawned widely and tossed his hair on 'lion', threw back his head and yodelled on 'wolf' and drew a crescent in the air for 'moon'. It was like watching a one-man band where you could not listen for fear that the player would do himself an injury. Would Puck manage without falling over?

Miss Ogle swallowed her own mirth, 'Do you want to share your thoughts with us, Annice?'

'No, Miss Ogle.'

'Take a break everyone, but don't leave the hall.'

She came towards us and frowned at the buckets which were set to catch drips from the ceiling. One was nearly full.

'Sam, will you empty that bucket, please?'

65

Sam took it away and manoeuvred the empty one into its place. The drip now sounded loudly in the hollow pail.

'What do you think of our Puck?' she asked me quietly.

'He's diabolical!'

She nodded.

'He is, isn't he?'

'Can't you have a word with him?' Heather asked.

'Oh,' Miss Ogle pulled a wry face, 'I know temperament when I see it.'

'At least he knows his lines,' Heather said.

'Yes, but I'll have to break the habit of miming before the performance. The ·bird impression is really too much!'

'Yes, why the bird?'

Miss Ogle shrugged.

'Ah well! On with the motley!'

She asked Puck to do his speech again and again he hopped winningly about the stage and this time even tried a few arm flaps.

'What bird is this?' Miss Ogle asked.

'The robin.'

'Robin is not a little redbreasted bird from a Christmas card,' she said with admirable restraint. 'He is Robin Goodfellow. Puck is Robin Goodfellow. He represents the spirit of the countryside.'

The boy looked mutinous. He stamped his little foot and then burst dramatically into tears.

'Oh dear!' Miss Ogle said, putting an arm on his shoulder. 'No need for that. Sit down on the stage everyone. I think that we need to talk.'

Sam and Heather sat with their backs to each other, leaning together, and I looked to see if Philip would expect me to do the same, but he threw a leg over a bench and sat astride it, so I sank to the floor on my own.

'It's not going well,' Miss Ogle said. 'Has anyone any idea why not?'

At first there was the usual silence and shuffling as everyone avoided her eyes and tried to force others to speak by staring at them. Eventually, the boy who was playing Bottom said, 'Why does there have to be so many things going on?'

'Shakespeare's plots seem difficult if you are used to stories where the writer describes the characters and the settings and then joins up the dots, but you know you recognize great casts of characters in soaps, and are perfectly capable of following more than one story-line at once. Think of it like an episode of *Coronation Street*. There's something going on in the Rover's Return that might be funny, at the same time as excitement in the corner shop, and at the same time as tragedy in one of the houses. In the same way there's the lovers in the wood, the magical world of the fairies and the comical world of Bottom and his friends.'

'But they get muddled up.'

'Sure they do, just like real life. None of you have just one thing going on at once. You're all sitting there listening to me, but that's not all that is happening to you. I'll bet that Heather is taking pleasure in the broadness of Sam's back and maybe also composing a shopping list.'

Heather blushed and shifted slightly.

'I'll bet that as I've been talking, a word has started up ideas in some of your minds quite beyond my intention. For example "television" might have started a train of thought about what you are doing this evening. If we could map the thoughts of everyone in the room, even for one minute, we'd find a tremendous range of ideas. Some writers ignore this and show their readers an easy path, a simple straight path, but the more they do this, the more unreal the story becomes. Good writers try to capture some of this richness. In the *Dream*, one of the things Shakespeare is doing is showing that his characters are quite capable of thinking of more than one thing at once, and so must you as an actor, and so must the audience.'

'But it's not just different groups of people in different parts of the wood, like it is in *Coronation Street*,' Philip said. 'Some of it is unreal. Some of them are away with the fairies!'

'Sure. It's an exploration of the imagination and the power of make-believe as much as it is anything else. But that's not so unreal, is it? Most of us daydream from time to time, don't we?'

'It's lies,' Philip said hotly, and then added, 'And it's dangerous. It's just not reasonable. It's not scientific!'

'The scientific method is very useful,' Miss Ogle conceded. 'I'm glad of all the benefits it's brought. It's a fine tool.'

Philip looked pleased. Then she added, 'In its place. Trying to understand people scientifically is like trying to butter bread with a scalpel.'

Miss Ogle looked round the stage and saw that we were dejected, drooping in a way more dramatic than anything we offered during the performance. She smiled and I smiled back.

'Your father, might he be able to help?'

'He's very busy,' I said quickly. I should have left it there but of course I wanted to please her so I continued, 'But maybe my cousin can help. Flora's at RADA but will be home for Easter. I could ask her if she would come and work with us, give us some ideas?'

The bench clattered as Philip clumsily shifted his weight. He caught my eye and shook his head slowly. It was as if he knew.

Heather and I were at the bus station.

'It's a pity you can't come after all, but your bus isn't for another half an hour, so shall we have a coffee?'

I should have been going to Heather's house but I could not face it. Why had I said that I had a cousin Flora at RADA? Why did I then have to make it worse by suggesting that she help at school? Now I was going to have to invent another set of circumstances to explain her non-appearance. What is the matter with me? I thought. Where's my self-control? I needed to get away, to be by myself.

'It's all right.'

'No bother. Come on.'

And so we sat in the dimly lit refreshment bar of the bus station. It must have once been bright and clean, but now the formica tables were chipped, the leatherette seats were either slashed or very dirty, and the walls, gloss painted in a custard colour, were covered with witless graffiti. An old man shuffled up and down the aisles talking to no one in particular. He was wearing an odd assortment of clothes and trying to catch somebody's eye, anybody's eye. I concentrated on my coffee. It was lukewarm and grey.

Heather warmed her hands on her mug of Bovril and took healthy slurps.

'That's better,' she said.

A woman at the corner table was muttering to herself and rummaging in endless carrier bags. Heather smiled at her and the mumbling stopped.

'Phil's a pain,' she said.

'Mm . . . Mm.'

'Shall I have a word with Sam?'

'No! I mean, what could you say?'

'I could tell him that you fancy Philip. He could sound him out for you.'

'No!' I almost shouted. 'No, Heather! Definitely not!'

'Okay.'

I tried the coffee again. It was sandy and gritty but had no taste except for the fattiness of the whitener.

'You know, for someone so bright he can be really stupid,' Heather went on.

'How do you mean?' I asked encouragingly, because I wanted her to go on talking about him, of course. I wanted an excuse to say 'Philip'. Philip. To hear 'Philip'.

'Well, he's a fool where other people are concerned, isn't he?'

'So am I.'

'Yes. You're a right pair,' Heather agreed good-naturedly. 'My grandmother says that he's too immersed in computers, but then she thinks that computers are the invention of the devil. Aunt Madge says that he believes that the world is a binary system where everything is either nought or one, on or off, right or wrong, real or unreal.'

'Isn't it?'

'Of course not. We don't live in a black and white world. There's colour, lots of colours, lots of shades. Gran says that Philip doesn't understand this. She says that he knows about rational and irrational, but not about non-rational.'

'Non-rational?'

'You know. Things that are nothing to do with reason at all.'

'I'm not sure that I do.'

'Well, Gran can explain it better.'

'I'd like to meet your grandmother.'

'Are you sure that you can't come?'

'The rehearsal was too long. They're expecting me at home and this is the last bus.'

'Could you phone?'

'No, there'll be no one there yet. I'm sorry not to see the dresses.'

'What about staying the night? I was really looking forward to you coming.'

'I can't. My parents are giving a party and I have to be there.'

'Another time then,' Heather said quietly, but I could see that she was hurt.

I let myself into the house and hung my coat on the pegs in the hall. I took out the library book. My father's greatcoat was there but not my mother's mac. I trudged up the stairs.

'Hello! I'm back.'

There was no answer. I went to the door of my father's room and pushed it gently open. His drawing board was now flat and he was bent over it delicately gluing a painted piece of paper into place. The drawing for the set of *A Midsummer Night's Dream* was now being translated into a model of the most incredible complexity.

'That's lovely,' I said.

He took off his glasses and peered at me. He always looked so stupid while his eyes were refocusing, so vacant, so vulnerable.

'There are still some problems but we're getting there.'

I was irritated by the 'we' when no one was working on it with him. I suppose that saying 'we' gave it some dignity, made it seem as though there was a real team involved, a team of designers, carpenters, electricians, painters, and set dressers, not just a frustrated ticket manager fooling about in an attic. I knew that I was

71

being unfair because my father was a trained set designer, but somehow he failed to get or to keep designing jobs in the theatre. His ideas were too complicated, too impractical, too out of fashion. What directors and managers wanted was discreet backdrops before which stars could shine. 'Minimalist' my father called them. Minimalist: the word was mean and ugly. I put my arms round his neck and hugged him.

'We're doing *A Midsummer Night's Dream* at school,' I said.

'That's nice.'

'I'm Hermia.'

'That's nice, poppet.'

I sometimes wondered if he called me 'poppet' and 'honey' and 'pet' because he could not remember my name in time. I ran my finger gently over the paper flats.

'Maybe we could build your set. What do you think?'

'In a school?' he said with such derision that I flinched.

'Well, maybe some part of it?'

'No,' he said huffily. 'It needs a big deep stage, not a school hall. It's all or nothing.' He sounded more insulted than angry.

'I'm sorry,' I said. 'I just thought that you might like to see it in use.'

He had already begun manoeuvring another flat into place, his big hands delicately tying off the thread from which it was suspended.

'Mum not back yet?' I asked.

'Has she gone out?'

'She's working today, remember?'

'That must be it then.'

He picked up a paint brush cut to leave only two or three hairs and began to colour yet another piece for the model.

'Dad, you know that I've been going to the art gallery most afternoons?' I did not wait for a reply but went on, 'I can get through one of the paintings to a garden. Something terrible is happening there. There was a fire, a girl got crippled, and it feels . . . it feels . . . creepy.'

I waited.

'What a pity, dear.'

'But didn't you hear what I said? I can go into a painting! I listen to the people. I'm actually there! It's summer at Caffelmeade.'

'That must be nice, honeybunch.'

'I'm leaving home. I'm running away with Mr Watson.'

'That's nice.'

'M-I-S-T-E-R Mister W-A-T-S-O-N Watson,' I said steadily but loudly.

My father looked up.

'Could you make me a coffee, Annie?'

I went down to the kitchen and filled the kettle. I knew that at any moment I would cry. I put coffee beans into the electric grinder and pressed down the switch in the lid. Under cover of the noise I allowed myself one sob.

'Stupid!' I said aloud.

Now I had upset Heather and for what? For something that was not even real.

I picked the library book up and shook it. One of the postcards that I had bought of the painting of Caffelmeade fell out. Philip was right. Making believe was dangerous, dreaming was a waste of time. I pounced on the card and tore it in half. The tear went raggedly down the side of the house and through the group. It looked like a hanging vine, a liana. Separating the halves, I moved David and Rosie and the cat away from the others. I plunged the coffee and sniffed.

'Are you quite sure that you don't want a big party for your birthday?' Elizabeth asked Flora, pouring the coffee into a filter.

They were having breakfast in the kitchen.

'I think that I would like it to be quite small. I would like just you and Matt and Rosie and maybe David.'

Elizabeth thought ruefully that David had been added as an afterthought, but this was a thin disguise. She knew that soon he was going to ask formally for her daughter's hand or to court her, or whatever they called it these days, and she sighed. They were so young! She still thought of them as children. David was at university and looked set to become a good scientist, but even if he became an eminent one, here he remained the gardener's nephew and if he wanted to court the daughter of the house, he felt that he needed her mother's permission. The Bennetts had been gardeners at Caffelmeade as long as the Wolsingtons had owned it. Matt had more right to call the place home than she had. He had been born to it, she had merely married it. Flora was sixteen! And so sure of herself! She scraped congealed egg and scraps of bacon from the pan into a plastic dish and then filled it with cat food from a tin. She took it to the door.

I had been standing in the doorway but now I seemed to be over by the window.

Elizabeth came back with a similar dish full of fish heads.

'Have you seen Grisaille lately?' she asked. 'She hasn't eaten yesterday's food.'

'Not for a few days,' Flora answered.

Rosie shook her head, her mouth full of bacon, running with egg yolk. Elizabeth tipped the fish into the rubbish and began to wash the dish.

'She's getting a bit old to go a-roving,' she said.

'She hardly brings any mice home now, just the occasional vole.'

'She's moving a lot slower,' Flora agreed. 'How long do cats live?'

'I think that twelve is a good age,' Elizabeth answered.

'How old is Grisaille?' Rosie asked.

'Matt gave her to me on my third birthday,' Flora answered.

'So, nearly thirteen,' Elizabeth murmured and then saw her younger daughter's lip quiver. 'But I'm sure that she will walk back in with her tail in the air. She always does, Rosie. Look, can't you persuade Flora to have a proper party. She'll regret it if she doesn't.'

'Sixteen's so old,' Rosie said dismissively.

'Thank you, baby.' Flora pulled a face at Rosie who went on eating undisturbed.

'But sixteen's an important birthday,' Elizabeth said.

'All right!' Flora gave in. 'But I don't want a big fuss.'

That seemed to settle the matter and they fell quiet. Then Elizabeth asked, 'How many? About a hundred?'

'I don't even know that many people!'

'Do you want a band?'

'No!'

'Live music's so much nicer.'

'Where would we put them?'

'A marquee?'

Flora said nothing but her looks were withering.

They were silent again.

'Perhaps fancy dress?' Elizabeth asked.

'Mother!'

Elizabeth held her hands up in mock defence. The windows rattled and they turned to see Matt looking in. Elizabeth opened the window.

'I think that you'd better come to see this,' he said. 'Will you come round to the stove house?'

He was waiting by the door.

'It's not a pretty sight,' he warned them.

I found that I had preceded them into the damp heat.

'What happened to them?' Elizabeth asked, looking at the bloated leaves of the giant pitcher plant. They were covered in a thick grey dust, and the small growths that would have been the pitchers in late summer were throbbingly bulbous.

'A disease,' he said, 'a very specific disease.'

'We'll send a specimen to the university,' Flora suggested, deftly manoeuvring her chair to the bench. 'They can identify it.'

Matt put a distorted plant into a polythene bag and gave it to her.

'If you want,' he said, 'but they can't bring them back.'

He took a bill-hook and began to pull down the crippled plant. The distorted, grotesque shapes of the embryo pitchers, swollen and hardened, hit the ground with dull thuds. I looked up and began to shiver. I found that I could not cry out, although I had seen Grisaille's tail high in the air. As though in slow motion Matt reached up and pulled the pitcher down and the remains of the cat fell to the floor, it's fur wet and clumped by a dark greenish-red ooze.

I thought, Oh, Esther, why did you bring the filthy thing here?

'I'm so sorry,' Matt said. 'She must have climbed up and fallen in.'

But in my mind, I saw the giant pitcher reach down and scoop up the cat who was too old and too slow to run. Maybe there was no disease, maybe the pitcher had died of indigestion.

76

I shivered in the tropical humidity, the cold coming from inside, only my hands were warm where I held the coffee pot. It had cooled but my father would hardly notice.

I gathered up the fragmented picture. My stories were no longer good stories. My stories were starting to bite back.

9

*A palynologist can analyse a core sample from the
ground and tell us which plants grew a hundred, five
hundred, a thousand years ago.*

I left the coffee and hurried to my room, taking the
stairs two at a time. He would probably forget that he
had asked for it anyway! I switched on the fire and
threw myself on to the bed pulling my jigsaw coat over
me. I still held the bits of the postcard in my hand. Now I
thrust them deep into the pockets of the coat. I would go
no more to Caffelmeade. I was done with it. You can
pretend for a very long time but when it starts falling apart
the fall is very swift.

The evening stretched interminably before me. Perhaps
I would go to Heather's house after all, and as I looked
for the number in the telephone book I worked on a story
to explain how I could get out into the country and back
again in so short a time. It was one thing to decide not
to pretend any more and another to work myself out of
the web in which I was already tangled. I could say that
David was driving into town to go to the theatre and had
offered me a lift. I was not sure that I had mentioned
David before but I could explain that he was our
gardener's nephew who was at university and that he
worked for us at weekends and in the college holidays.
That would be all right.

I had found the number and was about to dial when
I remembered that I had said that my parents were

giving a party and that I had to be there. I let the telephone directory close. It was no good. I had talked myself into a corner. I could not go to Heather's without yet more invention.

I heard the front door open and close. My mother had come home. I heard footsteps up to the workroom and then the low murmur of conversation. Almost immediately the front door opened and closed again. My father had returned to the theatre. On Saturdays and Wednesdays he went to both performances. I went to look at my books in the hope that I might find one that I had not read for some time. In a while my mother would call me for a meal and then the evening would have to be got through until a late supper when my father returned. My mother would probably watch television. I found myself wondering what they all did on a Saturday evening. Were Heather and Sam at the pictures? Where was Philip? Was he three rows behind with 'Titania', Elspeth's long blonde hair on his shoulder? I knew what Flora and David did on Saturday nights, but then I knew what they did all the time, didn't I?

'I saw you on Sunday with your mother,' Heather said to me as we waited in line for the school cafeteria.

'Where?' I asked.

'At the supermarket.'

I hesitated. I would have liked to deny it but if Heather had seen me clearly then there was not much point.

'Oh yes,' I said as though just remembering.

'It's a long way to come to shop,' Heather remarked.

'We ran out of ordinary things. You know what it's like after a party. Plenty of caviare and custard but nobody remembered the bread and the milk. Shops don't open in our area on a Sunday.'

Heather seemed satisfied.

'Your mother's not like I thought she would be,' she continued. 'She's very glamorous, isn't she?'

I remembered that my mother had been dressed for show. She was working for a businessman who liked to hold Sunday afternoon conferences and also liked the cachet of a PA both older and more sophisticated than his usual typist. My mother had therefore been swanning through Tesco's in an Italian pink coat with a mock grey-fox collar and an imposing cossack hat. Suddenly it seemed flashy and tawdry and I had a picture of Elizabeth Wolsington in soft camel.

'Oh,' I said, 'that wasn't my mother. It was my mother's secretary.'

'Your mother has a secretary?'

'Not all the time! Only at weekends, for the book.'

The queue had moved while we were talking and we were now being jostled from behind. There had been no need for that, I thought, no need at all. There's nothing wrong with my mother, nothing at all. She's a perfectly ordinary woman. I panicked. It was going to be difficult to keep my new friends from meeting my family. They would start to think it odd that they were never invited home with me and might just call uninvited. Then I remembered that we lived far away in the country and felt more secure. I would not be asking them home.

'Miss Ogle was there too,' Heather now said, 'buying fat-free yoghurts.'

They say that eavesdroppers never hear good of themselves. Philip would no doubt say that this was 'statistically unsupportable', but it was true for me that day. The first bit of listening-in happened by accident.

The noise in the staffroom was as bad as in the dining hall but of a different quality. There was no clattering of cutlery, no crashing of crockery, but there was a cacophony of challenging voices, a radio tuned to the racing at Doncaster and, on and off, bursts of Beethoven as someone tried to find the place on a cassette. The air was curiously thick and dusty although this was a smoke-free zone and the school used whiteboards and markers. It was as though the decades of chalk using, tobacco belching teachers had left a permanent inheritance in the very air that their successors breathed.

I did not know the procedure for winkling a teacher out of the staffroom. In some of my schools you just walked in and right up to them, in others you knocked and waited at the door; at one, you sent in a note and then retired to the far end of the corridor. Just what was expected here?

There were two doors into the room set opposite each other and both were propped open. I saw Miss Ogle come in through the other door with a pile of report books and look around for somewhere to sit. The staffroom was crowded, hence the open doors. There was room for about one third of the school's teachers, but then I suppose teachers should not sit down for more than one third of their day.

'Here,' Mr Watson called, lifting his bag on to the floor, 'you can perch here, but I don't think that I can find you any table space.'

Mr Watson said this with a display of annoyance, speaking louder than was necessary. The four teachers playing poker heard him but ignored him.

'I wouldn't mind so much if it was bridge,' he added.

'Thanks,' Miss Ogle said. 'I'll write on my lap. What the parents think of my handwriting I can't imagine!'

'Do you think they read them?'

'Oh yes! Surely.'

81

'Oh dear! I rather work on the assumption that they don't.'

Miss Ogle settled down to draft the reports. I knocked on the door but no one took any notice. Teachers went in and out brushing past me, but no one asked what I wanted. I was just going to go in and present myself when I heard, 'What do you make of Annice Campbell?'

I should have made myself known then, of course I should, but I did not. I retreated to the corridor and I listened.

'Is that the new girl? The one I suggested for Hermia?'

'Yes.'

'She's a flake.'

Miss Ogle laughed. It was such an odd word to hear delivered in Mr Watson's level expressionless voice, such an odd word for him to use at all.

'A flake?'

'Yes, you know, "kookie", "weird", "odd", a "screwball".' As he said this I'm sure that he made quotation marks in the air.

'Why do you say that?'

'You do mean the small girl with the mass of plum-coloured hair and the patchwork clothes?'

'Yes.'

'Need I say more?'

'There something strange going on. Her Mock results are quite mediocre. She only got a bare D from you for English and yet she seems so bright and so well read when we're doing *The Dream*, and look at all these books! She is well read. Mind you it's a strange sort of list.'

I realized then that she was looking at our reading lists. Each pupil here was obliged to keep a list of their personal reading with short comments beside each entry.

I had filled in pages and pages in the few weeks that I had been at the school. Mr Watson glanced down at it.

'It's long!'

'Yes, but not only that. I get lists that have been well thought out by the canny ones who only record what they know to be worthy, whether they've read them or not, and I also get long lists of rubbish from those who either know no better or who are honest. I don't usually get lists this long that are so uneven. She reads anything and everything. There are books in there that I would have thought way outside her interest or ability and also stuff that's the worst kind of tripe.'

'Maybe she's a compulsive reader.'

'Then why doesn't she do better at English?'

'If I remember correctly, she's undisciplined and self-indulgent. Her answers are packed with material but it's not ordered and of little relevance to the questions. She presents a ragbag of ideas, nothing more.'

'You mean she lacks judgement?'

'I mean that she has verbal diarrhoea!'

'She writes a lot?'

'Oh yes! Reams!'

'She's a puzzle!'

'Do you think that she's actually read them all?' Mr Watson asked.

'Do you know, I hope not. I never thought that I would say that, but if she's reading at this rate and so haphazardly she's in danger of emotional overload.'

Two teachers went past me but said nothing. They probably assumed that I had been asked to wait. When I tuned in again Miss Ogle was saying, 'And all books give us new experiences, whether they are good books or bad books or mediocre books. When we read we are feeding our memories, at second hand, certainly, but sometimes more vividly and always with more speed and physical ease than the real experiences would take.'

'I suppose so. Yes.'

'Then it's possible to become addicted to this quick-fix way of building memory, sort of living through the printed word, isn't it?'

'It might be I suppose if you read without intelligence, just swallow it in an undigested lump.'

'But you said yourself that that's just what Annice does do. She doesn't analyse anything, just takes it in and regurgitates it. It's possible to get high on literature. For some people poetry does the trick, for others science fiction.'

'Oh, but you're talking about books as though they're a drug!'

'Yes I am,' she replied.

So that's it, I thought, that's why my daydreaming has got out of hand; I have read too much and too quickly and got in a muddle. Yet, even as I thought it I did not really believe it.

The second overheard conversation was between Philip and Heather. We rehearsed in groups for an hour after school each day. It had been decreed by the head teacher that no pupil should spend more time on the play than on revising for the GCSE. We each spent, therefore, two hours a week rehearsing. We thought the arithmetic faulty. Few of us were yet revising at all and none daily, but it must have been a good scheme anyway because the play and players had quite suddenly found each other. Hoots of laughter could be heard on the days when the 'mechanicals' met and only slightly less when the fairies began their flying lessons. They were to climb and sway on a series of ropes and swings. None of the moves choreographed by Miss Ogle were in themselves difficult but it took them some time to fit them together and in the meanwhile they collided and tangled and more often than not ended up in a giggling mass on the stage.

'This is one thing I can't help you with,' Miss Ogle said. 'There's nothing on earth would get me up on a rope and the swing hasn't been built that can take my weight.'

While this was happening on the stage I was sitting in the wings reading.

'What's your problem?' It was Heather, talking quietly on the other side of the flat.

'What do you mean?'

Philip.

'What's wrong with Annie?'

'Nothing really.'

'Nothing really?'

'Well,' he said, 'she's not easy to talk to.'

'I have no problem.'

'Oh yes you do! She's like a turtle with a very thick shell. You spend a lot of time coaxing her out.'

'Is that all?' Heather asked.

'Well, if you must know, and remember you asked for it, she moons about. She strikes poses. She's a fake.'

'What do you mean?'

'I don't want to talk about it.'

'Well I do!' Heather said angrily. 'You can't say something like that and then just walk off. She's my friend.'

Then Philip said diffidently, 'I've seen it all before, Heather. My mother was like her.'

Heather said nothing and as the silence lengthened, the tension grew. Then she said, 'I don't know what to say. I didn't know that you remembered your mother. Sam has never said.'

'I was eight. You can be quite grown up at eight if you have to be.'

'And she was like Annie?'

'She read all the time when I was little, always carrying a book, just like she does.'

'And you do,' Heather pointed out.

He ignored this.

'All I can remember is her hands and the back of a book. I can't really remember her face. She would make up stories about people on the bus or in cafés. You know the kind of thing? The man in the fur hat was a Russian spy, the couple at the next table were eloping, running away from her cruel father, the old lady on the park bench was really a Polish princess who had been lost as a baby.'

'There's no harm in that!' Heather said. 'I often make up stories about people, doesn't everyone?'

'I don't!'

'What's this got to do with Annie?'

'She stands there in her strange clothes and she smiles and she talks, but she's somewhere else.'

'What happened to your mother?' Heather asked gently.

'She was killed by a bus,' he said harshly. 'She was probably day-dreaming.'

I heard Heather's intake of breath. Then, 'But Annie's nice when you get to know her. Why don't you give her a chance? At least stop being so stubborn about the play.'

'Stubborn?'

'You might fool Miss Ogle, but I know that you can't possibly be so bad at acting. No one can!'

'Sh!' Miss Ogle hissed. 'Stop whispering behind the scenes!'

I tried to read again, dipping into the gardening book.

It is said that the pollen of the asphodel, the immortal flower which grew in Elysium, blinded the gods to reality. It is certain that care must be taken when analysing pollen samples for some plants produce a mock pollen to attract insects, but it is merely good imitation.

I searched the index of the flower book. There it was. *'Asphodoline lutea* (asphodel)'. I knew really before I found the page, knew that it would show me a tall spike of yellow star-shaped flowers and narrow green leaves, for I had met the asphodel once, at Caffelmeade, and felt the effect of its pollen in my eyes. Then I knew that I was not just dreaming about what I had read. That would not explain this, for this time the dream came first.

'Annie!'

'Annie!' Miss Ogle called again, then 'Annice!'

I looked up.

'We're ready to start. Do you mind me calling you Annie?'

'No,' I answered, 'I'm Annie in town and Annice in the country.'

The rehearsals for the lovers were of a more sober nature but even so the atmosphere had lightened. It had lightened for one reason only and that was because Philip, stung by Heather, had started to act. The words no longer choked him and he said them with meaning.

> *'I mean that my heart into yours is knit;*
> *So that but one heart we can make of it.'*

'That's more like it,' Miss Ogle said when we had finished the scene. 'Yes. That's really quite nice.'

Heather nudged me and whispered. I shook her off but blushed even so.

'He's pretending, Heather. It's the part, for heaven's sake!'

'Are you sure?'

'Certain sure.'

'Well done, Philip,' Miss Ogle continued. 'Yes, really well done. You've started to get the way of it. You've started to act.'

'Against my better judgement,' Philip answered.

10

In 1642 as King Charles I left London and set up his battle standard in a field outside Nottingham John Trandescant Junior was visiting America collecting specimen plants. By the time Prince Rupert led his cavalry against Cromwell at Edgehill, he had returned bringing with him a plant that was to change the face of England as surely as the Commonwealth. The Virginia creeper, Parthenocissus quinquefolia, *had arrived to disguise, ornament, and disfigure.*

The second phase had begun. I knew now that something was happening apart from my daydreaming, something outside myself, and I began to look for an explanation. Miss Ogle had blamed undigested reading, but I had already moved on to something much more exciting. There was only one person I could ask, only one person that would not laugh.

At school the next day I sought him out. I found Philip sitting in the physics prep room. Well, it was called the physics prep room because that is what it said on the door, but it was really little more than a store cupboard. He was perched on a lab stool which he had tipped back on two legs so that he could rest his shoulders against the wall. He was reading a thick, dull-looking book. I reminded myself that he was, or should have been, the school swot. There's no justice in the world.

I pulled out a lab stool, positioned it next to him and nonchalantly threw myself back. The legs shot away.

'You need to be closer to the wall. You have to work out the fulcrum,' Philip said as I gathered my dignity together.

'Right,' I said, and then, as casually as I could, 'Is time travel possible?' I sat squarely on the stool and dangled one leg in what I hoped was a sophisticated manner. He had gone back to his book. I sneezed.

'Have you got a cold?' he asked, as though it was the plague. 'I can't afford flu with the match on Saturday.'

Rugby! I have often noticed that very fit people have poor health. It is some consolation.

'No. I don't think so. What about time travel? Is it possible?'

'Maybe,' he said without looking up from the book.

'Would it be possible to kind of boomerang back and forth through time?'

'Well, it has been suggested.'

Another page turned. Philip said 'well' often. He said it as though delivering the final word in an argument.

'What would it be like?'

Philip closed his book and looked at me.

'Why the sudden interest in physics?'

'I just wondered.'

'You mean H. G. Wells stuff?'

I managed to look blank because I knew that there was nothing boys like Philip liked better than explaining things, unless of course it was converting a try.

'H. G. Wells was an author,' he began and I tried to look suitably fascinated to encourage him. Oh, how easy it was! 'He wrote a book about a time machine.'

'No machine,' I interrupted before he could launch

himself into a full résumé of the book. 'Just a sort of slip, as if a person who's alive today might be able to go back and sort of observe the past.'

'Like a spectator?'

'Yes. No.'

'Make up your mind.'

'It's difficult to explain.'

'Well, it's funny that you should ask me that right now, because I've been wondering about something for a bit, but it's just an idea of my own. I've never seen it anywhere.'

'Go on.'

'Well, there may be hyperstrings sort of floating about.'

This time I looked blank with no effort at all.

'Well, I made the name up. You know about cosmic strings?'

I shook my head.

'Philip, don't swing on two legs like that, you'll break the stool. And just look at that greasy mark on the wall.'

Philip slowly settled the stool back on four legs as Mr Smithers came into the room. Mr Smithers was the newest member of staff, fresh from college and full of goodwill towards pupils. He flung himself on to the stool beside Philip and settled his back against the wall. Philip smiled and rocked back again himself.

'Hyperstrings?' Mr Smithers prompted.

'Cosmic strings,' Philip told me, 'are, or rather were, rifts in space-time. In one theory, they explain how the universe expanded. They're a bit like geological fault lines in rocks, but in space and time.'

I know that I looked blank. He tried again.

'It's where space-time got out of line and these rifts allowed the universe to expand. This was in the inflationary period, of course.'

It was hard to tell if Philip was pulling my leg, but Mr Smithers did not laugh and so I said, 'Of course.'

'They don't exist any more,' Philip went on. 'They drifted about in the primordial universe.'

'What about hyperstrings then?' Mr Smithers asked with apparently genuine interest.

'Well,' Philip said, and blushed, 'supposing remnants of these cosmic strings are still around, little threads disjointing space and time, still wandering. If there are, then it might be possible to slip through, or rather be pulled through to a different time and a different place.'

'What would it feel like?' I asked.

Philip shrugged.

'Let's think about it,' Mr Smithers said. 'There'd be a big disturbance, of course.'

'Light?' I ventured.

'Brightness, I would say, wouldn't you, Philip? Yes. Pure. Pure brightness.'

'How would you feel yourself?' I asked.

'You'd have zero length,' Mr Smithers answered.

'And it would also seem as though you were stretched to infinity,' Philip jumped in.

'You'd feel nowhere and everywhere?' I suggested.

Philip beamed.

'Sure. That's right.'

'Could you return to your own time?'

Philip hesitated.

'Yes,' Mr Smithers said. 'If the hyperstring crossed you again.'

'What about your own time?'

They looked enquiringly at me.

'How much time would pass? How much real time?'

'"Real" doesn't mean much when you're dealing with this kind of thing.'

'How much of your own time?' I repeated.

'Any amount,' they both said.

'None?'

'Perhaps. Yes. It could be instantaneous.'

'Then this might be happening all the time. Are you saying that we couldn't detect it?'

They thought for a while and then Philip said, 'It might be a bit like the subconscious.'

Mr Smithers nodded.

'What?' I asked.

'Well,' Philip said, 'you can never prove that you have a subconscious because you can only know this consciously.'

'You can't sort of catch yourself thinking subconsciously,' Mr Smithers said helpfully.

'Then your hyperstrings can never be proved,' I said. I was disappointed.

'So what?'

'Then they're just imaginary. Not part of science?'

They both laughed.

'But you said yourself, Philip, that you're only interested in facts. You can't build on something that you can never prove exists.'

'Freud did,' Mr Smithers replied.

I had to ask one more question.

'What would make this happen?'

'Accident,' Philip said. 'Someone, or something, just getting snagged.'

'Then you can't make it happen?'

'Harness it?' Philip asked. 'Now that's an interesting idea . . .'

'Suppose . . .' Mr Smithers said, and they were away trading theories like you might trade marbles, building towering universes out of nothing, walking where I could not follow. I let them talk, but there was nothing more that made any sense to me.

As the bell rang I asked, 'If someone got sucked back by a hyperstring . . .'

'Or forwards?'

'Or sideways?'

'Whatever. If they did? Would they know?'

Mr Smithers looked at me kindly.

'It's only an idea. We're only playing a "What if" game. It couldn't really happen to you.'

'Why not?'

'Because you'd be dead. You'd be crushed under your own infinite mass.'

'To say nothing of the annihilation of the solar system when the string whipped through!' Philip laughed.

Scientists want us to think that they are practical, but that is just to put the rest of us off their track. Scientists, I was dimly beginning to realize, deal in mystery. I did not for one minute believe in Philip's 'hyperstrings', but they did have an attractive kind of logic that would explain my involuntary journeys to Caffelmeade. I wanted an explanation that was outside myself and so the idea seeded itself in my mind.

It was Saturday morning and the cast had assembled so that costumes could be fitted. A changing room made by standing three screens against the wallbars had been erected in the hall and a standing mirror wheeled in from the domestic science room.

'You will each come forward in turn and put on your costumes and then go up on to the stage so that we can see what they look like from a distance,' Miss Ogle said. 'While you are waiting try not to make too much noise. You could perhaps learn your lines.'

I was worried about the costumes and ready to be apologetic. However, when Heather's mother carried the boxes into the hall she was looking pleased.

'They're not bad,' she said to Miss Ogle. 'Not as good as the drawings, but not bad.'

First she brought out armfuls of silk in every colour and shade imaginable and piled them on the floor. She plunged her hand into the heap, a quick shake, and there was Hermia's dress. She picked up the remaining bundle and with the same flick of the wrist shook out Helena's costume. They were made in the same way with close-fitting bodices and multi-layered skirts, but where Hermia's was spring in blue, yellow, and green, Helena's was summer in red, orange, and pink.

'They haven't got any fasteners yet. I couldn't bring myself to put anything as heavy as a zipper into them. Maybe I'll just sew up the back seam by hand once you have them on. There are no changes, are there?'

We went behind the screen and put them on.

'I don't think that we can wear much under them,' Heather said. 'Mum wouldn't let me try it on at home in case it looked silly on me. Sam saw it while she was machining it and he said that it looked like the big rock candy mountain.'

'Well it doesn't,' I reassured her. 'More like gossamer than candyfloss.'

We emerged from behind the screen clutching our hands to our backs.

'I'll just pin them for now,' Mrs Hindle said, bearing down on us with a mouthful of glass-headed pins.

When she had finished she sat back on her heels.

'Well, what do you think?'

'I think that they look wonderful,' Miss Ogle said. 'Up on to the stage with you. How did you manage it on our budget?'

'I went to the market. It's only lining stuff, you know. It has no goodness in it.'

95

'It has now,' Miss Ogle said twiddling her finger in the air so that we would pirouette.

'Could they be laced together at the back?' I asked, remembering Flora in her dress of spring flowers.

'Why of course. That's the answer! I'll put really thin rouleau laces in. Why didn't I think of that?'

After that I relaxed. It was going to be all right. The stage was filling with colour and glitter. Only Bottom was left to be dressed.

'I wasn't sure about the ass's head,' Mrs Hindle said. 'The drawing is so clever. It makes him look cute but also something else.'

'Sexy,' Miss Ogle said without hesitation. 'If you look at the drawing, this is a cuddly animal but it's also a man with a leer.'

'Well, what do you think of this?' she asked and brought a papier mâché creation out of the last box. It had huge soft silver furry ears that were so irresistible that both Miss Ogle and Bottom put their hands out to stroke them. But the mask also had a sickening smile, both silly and dangerous. Bottom put it on. He turned to go up on to the stage and everyone fell silent. Then there was a nervous giggle from one of the fairies.

'Behold!' Miss Ogle said grandly. 'Bottom the Weaver transformed.'

The cast were still quiet except the boy who was playing Quince who heard himself say, *'Bless thee, Bottom! Bless thee! Thou art translated.'*—and understood it fully for the first time.

They don't like it! I thought. They don't understand it. They want a sweet donkey.

'You have them gob-smacked!' Miss Ogle said.

Then they all began to talk at once and to laugh and even to clap. Miss Ogle using slang was almost as wonderful as the ass's head.

'We've talked before about the dark side of *The Dream*,' she went on sensing an advantage. 'Well, now you see it. Thanks to Annice's father and Heather's mother we now have the underbelly of the play. Always remember that this is not a pretty safe English garden, it is a place where *"the snake throws her enamelled skin, Weed wide enough to wrap a fairy in."* While I've got you all up there we'll practise the curtain call. Some of you are stuck all over with pins so please be careful. Mrs Hindle and I'll do our best to clap for you. Now. Everyone to the side. Oberon, Titania, and their train have left. If you will give us the final passage, Puck, we'll go from there. You know the order.'

I stood at the side with Heather and Sam and Philip and waited for our turn to take a bow. Miss Ogle had decided that Helena and Demetrius would come in fractionally before Hermia and Lysander and that the couples would take separate bows and then all four together. I was nervous because I was not sure how Philip would behave and my imagination ran ahead. How would he cope with holding hands? I was used to touching him in the play, of course, but that was not really us, that was Hermia and Lysander. But this was different. This was after the play. Would he do it as though in character and then drop my hand instantly? Or would he, and this would be the most shaming of all, not even hold it in the first place?

Sam and Heather had already run to the front of the stage and bobbed their first quick acknowledgement to the audience of two. I held my breath. Philip grabbed my hand and forward we went. A quick bob and then back to join Heather and Sam, and then slowly forward still holding hands and a slower bow. Miss Ogle and Heather's mother kept on clapping, so Sam took my hand and we bowed once more as a foursome.

'Just a minute,' Miss Ogle said, 'You're supposed to be pleased at a job well done, Annice. You look as though you're going to your execution. Smile! Let's do it again.'

And so we went through it again, and I, knowing that Philip had kept hold of my hand through it all and did not look as though he was in any hurry to drop it, folded my fingers comfortably round his and smiled. All was well in the best of all possible worlds.

I was in my father's workroom trying to clean.

'Just flick a duster over it and hoover whatever floor is visible,' my mother had advised. 'He won't notice anyway.'

I lingered over the model set for *The Dream*. It was now about half complete and was already a dense tangle of fly-ropes and flats and gauzes. A money spider launched itself across the space. Even the floor of the stage had been painted with leaves and flowers and diamond-backed serpents.

'You spotted snakes with double tongue.'

It was Flora's voice. She was outlining with her fingers the twists of the iron locks on the heavy oak doors.

I saw that we were inside Caffelmeade. Flora, her mother, David, and Rosie were crowded round a door. I knew that it was winter.

'It hasn't been open for as long as I can remember,' Elizabeth said holding up a great key. 'This may not even be the right key. Do you want to do it, David? It'll be rusted.'

David took the key.

'It fits,' he said and he turned it easily and pushed very gently with his index finger. The five foot wide door swung open and Rosie laughed nervously.

'I expected some creaking of old hinges, or scraping of swollen wood,' Elizabeth said, expressing the thoughts of all.

'Ah, wood like this was properly seasoned,' David explained. 'Do you want to look first?'

We filed into the first room but could see nothing.

'It sounds empty,' Flora declared.

David switched on a small pocket torch and using the tiny beam to make sure that his way was clear went to the window wall.

'If you give me a hand, Flora, we can open the casements.'

Flora reached up from her chair and tugged at the bottom while David prised open the top.

They proved less smooth than the door and rewarded us with a great deal of creaking and groaning. The thin winter light filtered in through the dirty glass to reveal that the room was indeed empty, or nearly so. It was panelled in oak with a wood-block floor of a crazy tessellating pattern. The only thing there was a small rough footstool.

'Let's see the second room,' Elizabeth suggested.

This opened with the same ease, but this time David had to negotiate Flora's chair around furniture to get to the windows.

'Oh dear, more oak,' Flora sighed, when they could see properly.

'I think that these are important pieces of furniture,' David said, first blowing and then carefully wiping the dust from a cupboard. 'I've seen some like these at Hampton Court.'

'But it's quite ugly,' Flora moaned, 'and we have so much heavy old wood. It makes me tired to look at it. I hoped that we might find something prettier.'

Flora was a foot away from David and I saw their

hands reach to come together as though they were marionettes on the same string. I remembered holding Philip's hand and remembered that he had not relinquished it until we had to part to struggle out of our costumes.

'Well, anyway, the room's not overflowing with rubbish and I think that some of the pieces would look well in the proper setting. Those that we do not want can be sold very profitably,' Elizabeth said crisply.

'Well, one last room,' Flora said.

The excitement had gone out of the group as they approached the last room. It now seemed obvious that the rooms had simply been locked because they were surplus to requirements. There was no hidden treasure, no walled up secrets, just a lot more dark panelling.

The door swung open on the last room and David's torch revealed bulky dustsheeted shapes before the light went out. The floor was soft and springy beneath my feet.

Carpet, I thought.

'I seem to be stuck,' Flora said. 'There's something tangled in my wheels.'

'The casements won't budge,' David called from the gloom, 'I'll fetch a light.'

'Mummy,' Rosie said, 'the floor isn't carpet, it's—'

'Rosie,' Elizabeth interrupted, 'don't go wandering about the room till we get the light, you might bump into something.'

'But, Mummy!'

Rosie had scarcely said this when there was a thump followed by a crash and then she howled.

'Where are you?' Elizabeth asked urgently.

'It's all right,' David said, 'I've got her. Stand up, Rosie. You're all right now.'

Rosie's howls died away to snuffles and the room went quiet again.

'I think that I can move this shutter after all. I can get my fingers behind it here.'

I heard the casement open as before, but this time no light came into the room. Elizabeth had felt her way towards David and now she reached out ahead of her to where the window should be. She screamed just as Matt arrived at the door with a storm lantern.

'It's all right,' David said. 'Look, it's just a creeper that's grown through from outside.'

'I tried to tell you,' Rosie said righteously.

'And so did I,' said Flora as she scraped leaves and tendrils from the spokes of her wheels.

Elizabeth opened her eyes slowly, willing herself not to scream again. The scream was turned into a sob. 'Something moved over my foot,' she whispered.

Everyone looked down. The Virginia creeper that was on the outside wall had found its way between the stone and had grown right over the window, under the casements, and across the floor. We were standing on leaves. Flora shuddered.

David started to pull away the dustsheets. They revealed a *bergère* day bed, its striped brocade looking fresh and bright, whilst the creeper twined in and out of the cane panels. Next a port table, the well in the centre bursting with vinery. Then a mirror. The creeper had wrapped around the wooden leaves and fruit on its frame, mocking the skill of the carver. On they went, removing sheet after sheet. Not a table leg or chair back were free of the tendrils which crept steadily up and over everything. Something slithered over a footstool and Elizabeth pointed wordlessly.

'And a thousand thousand slimy things
Lived on; and so did I,' came unbidden to my mind.

'Now there's a thing I've never seen before,' Matt said. 'Look how it's kept its leaves indoors and without light though it's bare outside at this time of year.'

'It's horrible,' Elizabeth said. 'Like a monstrous birthmark.'

'Oh, I don't know,' he said. 'It's a lovely red.'

I was staring once more at the model stage and the money spider had just landed. Instantaneous. No time had passed in my father's study. I was upset, but strangely no longer frightened. I had to tell Philip.

11

During the nineteenth century, as one by one the
alpine peaks fell to British climbers, so too did the
rock plants. Gentian, saxifrage, campanula,
eidelweiss, primula, were torn from the rich upland
meadows and rocky clefts, to adorn miniature
Matterhorns in suburban English gardens. One plant,
Eritrichium nanum, *the silver leaf borage, resisted,*
never survived transplantation.

I woke the next morning to happiness, not just the absence of unhappiness, but positive, undeniable, well-being. The joy swelled physically inside me, rapping at my ribs, catching my throat, making me want to jump and run and sing.

The day ahead was mapped out in my mind and all of it was satisfactory. I would go first to Heather's, then to the gallery at lunch time and have a toasted sandwich with Philip and then we would walk together to school and the dress rehearsal. After that the whole cast was going by coach to Brimham Rocks to see a promenade version of the play. I would sit with Philip. I would walk with Philip. It was like being inside a novel. The scenes were set, the characters had been drawn, all that was needed was to join up the dots and the familiar plot would be revealed. All the muddle was gone. It was as simple as 'boy meets girl' after all.

First I had to borrow my father's drawings for the stage set. He would not miss them because he now had the model. It was too late to build anything like it, of course, and anyway the hall had to be used for teaching until the day before the play, but there was still time to paint flats and to suspend some tie-dyed gauzes. Then I had to go to Heather's to help with the ironing and the packing. For the first time since moving into the house I was down in the kitchen making toast even before my mother's alarm had rung.

'Annie!' my mother exclaimed coming cautiously into the kitchen. She opened her sticky eyes wide, tied her dressing gown tighter and roughed up her hair. 'I'm not used to company this early on a Saturday!'

'Evidently!' I answered.

She made a rueful face and smiled.

'Just wait, my lady,' she said. 'Age does not mean that you can't stay up most of the night, but it does mean that you take longer to recover.'

'Where are you today?'

'Copy typing. Insurance company.'

'Poor you!'

'Why are you so cheerful this morning? You're not only up, but dressed!'

I was wearing a plain putty-coloured shift and thick tights in almost the same shade. On my feet I had flat two-toned brown loafers. There was no jewellery, no decoration of any kind and for once no Doc Marten boots. My hair still glowed like a Victoria plum but the dye was starting to grow out and fade a little. I had scraped it back behind a hair band so that my high forehead was revealed. I hoped that I looked like a ballet dancer in exercise clothes.

'Is this a new image or are you already in costume?'

'I felt like a change.'

'It's certainly that! Perhaps if you bring your hair forward. Soften it a bit.'

'This is how I want it.'

She shook her head and sighed.

'Annie, you don't even try to be like other girls. A gypsy yesterday and now a nun. How can you expect to fit in when you won't compromise?'

'Why should I?'

'The world has to take you or leave you on your terms, I suppose?'

I nodded. Mostly it left me. Now, however, I had Philip.

'Are you coming home to change before this evening?'

'No. I'm going to Heather's this morning, then to the rehearsal, and then straight on to the bus.'

'Like that?'

'I'm taking a rucksack, with jeans, a T-shirt, sweater, boots, and my coat.'

She was about to protest when I said, 'It's out of doors remember.'

I stood in the porch at Heather's house. The outer door was open, so I had walked in. The porch was a cube of glass and plastic stuck on to the front of an old brick semi. Tubs of spring bulbs, the flowers having given way to masses of foliage, stood around the floor, along with an assortment of wellington boots, wide down-at-heel shoes covered in mud, a trowel, and some seed packets. An aspidistra stood on a rickety cane table next to the front door. It shared its precarious perch with a sticky bottle of castor oil and a disreputable rag that had once been underpants. I had to reach through the leaves to ring the bell.

Heather opened the door. She was heat-curling her hair and one side of her face was framed by the familiar glossy yellow bell and on the other side her hair hung straight.

'I'm a bit early.'

'No. It's all right. This house is like Piccadilly Station this morning. Come in if you can get in,' Heather said.

I followed her into the narrow hall, made all the narrower by cardboard boxes stacked along the wall.

'You look different,' Heather said. 'Is that a new dress?'

'What this? I've had it for ages.'

'Mum's working in the front room,' Heather said, 'but come into the living room and have a drink first.'

I was taken into a room that I would have described as a kitchen. It had a cooker, a fridge, a sink, and a dining table but it also had a fireplace with a real fire, a sofa, two fireside chairs and a bookcase. Half the table was taken up with a giant aspidistra, twice the size of the one in the porch. A woman was standing at the table pouring water into seven mugs. She was old and dignified even though pink and blue foam curlers martialled her iron-grey hair into regimented rows across her scalp.

'This is Annice,' Heather said. 'Annie, this is my Aunt Madge. Well she's my great-aunt really but that's too much of a mouthful. She was an infant teacher, a headmistress actually. She was a Wren during the war. She lives in Scunthorpe. She's staying with us because it's my gran's birthday.'

'Good morning, dear,' Aunt Madge said. 'Now you know all that is even remotely interesting about me. Coffee?'

'Yes please.'

Aunt Madge gave me a mug and said, 'When you've finished crimping, Heather, we'll go up and see Maud.'

'Finished,' Heather said giving her head a shake.

'*Avanti!*'

I hesitated, not sure what I should do.

'Well come along, dear,' Aunt Madge said.

'Me too?'

'Yes. Maud likes a crowd in her bedroom. She will hold court like the French kings used to.'

I followed them up the stairway. The light from the window on the landing was obscured for a moment as Sam stood to one side to let us pass.

'Coffee's on the table. Tell the others, will you?' Aunt Madge said to him.

'Happy birthday, Gran,' Heather called, pushing wider the already open bedroom door. The bed was empty, only a faint depression in the pillow showing that it had been used. A leg rose slowly from behind it, an elegant satin pyjama terminated by a striped woollen bedsock.

'Thank you, Heather.'

Heather stretched across the bed and looked down at her grandmother who lay on the floor flexing her muscles.

'Gran, you're eighty today, remember!' Heather admonished gently.

'Maudie, what d'you think you're doing?' Aunt Madge asked.

'I know what I'm doing,' the old lady replied. 'Tell me, Madge, do school teachers learn to do that, or does it come naturally?'

'Do what?'

'Pretend to be indignant when they're not.'

Aunt Madge ignored this and offered her sister her hands.

'You don't like my pyjamas,' Heather's grandmother said, 'I can tell.'

'Reminds me of Jean Harlow,' Madge replied.

'Why, thank you!'

'But if she were still alive she wouldn't be wearing them!'

'More fool her! What should I wear, winceyette to the neck?'

'I do!' replied Madge as she hauled her sister up. They smiled in conspiracy, excluding the girls.

'It's my birthday, Madge.'

'How could we fail to know that, Maud?'

'Can I come in?'

I felt the hairs rise on the back of my neck and I almost spilled the coffee.

'Of course,' Heather's grandmother said. 'I never refuse a handsome man.'

Madge grunted and turned her eyes to heaven as Philip came into the room.

'Happy birthday,' he said and gave Maud a spindly two-leafed aspidistra. She took it as though it was precious and smiled.

'Come and help me with the washing,' Mrs Hindle called up the stairs. 'Those fairies have got their frocks mucky.'

Everyone laughed.

'Come on,' Aunt Madge said. 'Let's go. Let her get dressed.'

Heather's grandmother patted the edge of her bed. 'Talk to me for a bit?' she said to me. I had little choice but to sit.

'Mind you look after it,' Philip shouted back from the stairs, 'it has ambition.'

Heather's grandmother smiled.

'You're Annice?' she asked.

'Yes.'

'You don't look like they said.'

'I don't usually look like this.'

'He's a good boy.'

'Who?'

'Who? Why, Magnus Magnusson of course. Has Heather got it wrong? Aren't you sweet on him, then?'

Sweet? I thought.

'I can see you are! You blush quite prettily. I've not seen a blush like that for years.'

'He didn't even notice me,' I said.

'Oh yes he did. He's got a stiff upper lip even on the inside, that one. But he can be very romantic.'

'Philip?'

'Yes, Philip.'

I shook my head uncertainly, 'He only works with facts.'

'That so? He brought me this infant aspidistra. You'll have noticed that we have a few about the house? Well, that's because my husband used to work for the parks department in Rochdale and he looked after two big ones that were kept for when Gracie Fields came home. You know who Gracie Fields was? "The Biggest Aspidistra in the World"?'

'I've read *Keep the Aspidistra Flying*.'

'Yes. Well, when she came to Rochdale these aspidistras had to be wheeled on to the station platform, you see. He always brought them home to have their leaves oiled for the big occasion. Just after we were married, for the second time, that is, but that's another story, I somehow killed them off. I don't know what I did, but the things turned their toes up! It was very shaming for him. Anyway. We've always kept aspidistras since then. Philip knows that they grow slowly. It's an encouraging present for someone my age. Romantic but not practical. Only interested in facts! That one's kidding someone. He'll need encouragement, of course.'

I didn't know what to say.

'Now tell me about yourself,' the old lady said and settled back against her pillows.

Usually I hate being asked to talk like a performing parrot, but for some reason I found it easy to talk to Heather's grandmother. I started with small things, but soon, as though floodgates had been opened, I was telling her everything. I told her about the garden and about the people at Caffelmeade. I told her how I felt about losing control of my daydreams and how I thought that they might not be daydreams after all.

When I had finished she patted my hand and said, 'Yes. I see, dear.'

I was disappointed although I had not consciously expected her to give me an answer. I suppose that I had thought she might. There must be some consolation for being so old.

'I don't think you do,' I whispered.

'Yes. I do see,' she answered. 'But I don't know what you want from me.'

'Well, what do you think? Am I going mad?'

'You know you're not.'

'What's happening to me, then?'

'I'll tell you what I think if you want, but you mustn't just accept it, you know. It's only what I think.'

I nodded.

'I think that you've been too much alone. It's good to like one's own company, essential as you get older, but it's not good to be too solitary. If you are, and if you have the normal desire for company, then you invent your own. That's what you've done.'

'Then why can't I stop?'

'I'm not sure, dear. The hermits saw visions. It was one of the reasons that they lived like that. Hostages who are kept in solitary confinement say that the edges blur between reality and imagination. I'll bet that you go to this garden less and less as you make friends here. The thing is not to worry about it. It'll fade away.'

'Sure?'

'Certain! And in the meantime you have to concentrate on snaring your fella.'

'Maud,' Madge said, coming back into the room, 'behave yourself! You're wanted, Annie.'

'Have a happy birthday,' I whispered.

I almost danced down the stairs. I could hear Heather, Sam, and Philip somewhere beyond the living room. I called.

'We're in the back kitchen,' Heather called back. 'Just come through.'

I went through the living room and found them in a small lean-to annex at the back which housed a freezer, a washing machine, a drier, and the central heating boiler. They were sorting through costumes.

'There's a coffee going cold on the table,' I told them.

'That's John's,' Heather said.

'John?'

'My grandmother's boyfriend.'

Heather said it as though it was perfectly normal for an eighty year old to have a boyfriend. Perhaps it was. How was I to know? My family was myself and my parents. There were no grandparents, no uncles and aunts, no cousins. Never had I spent a morning in a house like this with people coming and going, with something happening in every room. So many people in such a small house yet I did not feel in the way, I felt accepted and at ease so that when Heather asked me to pop to the front sitting room and fetch her mother, it seemed natural to skip through the living room and down the hall.

I opened the sitting room door to be confronted by a rail of costumes. I parted them and was surprised to find myself walking down the gravel path at Caffelmeade. Flora was just ahead of me, wrapped in a mohair jacket.

The chair crunched on the gravel as she spun herself along. It was the coldest of February days when the steel grey sky lightens only to a thin opalescence at midday. The borders were desolate, last year's plants brown and grey, the remains of their leaves sodden, their stems twisted and rimed with frozen fog. The heated greenhouse was steamed. I could see Matt's fuzzy outline as he moved inside. Flora knocked at the door and he let her in.

'May I sit with you for a while?'

He poured her a coffee from his thermos flask.

'This reminds me of when I was little and you used to give me drinks and fetch me Battenberg cake. I wasn't supposed to eat between meals. Did you know that?'

'And you used to unroll the marzipan and then divide the cake into separate squares. You always ate the yellow ones first, then the pink ones and finally the marzipan. Then you used to lick each finger very slowly.'

He reached in his haversack and brought out a Battenberg cake wrapped in film. Flora laughed. She cut a slice and as she watched him working, she slowly dissected the cake and began with the yellow squares.

Matt was repotting the alpines. On his right were large boxes of plants removed from the rockeries. He was dividing and rehousing them ready to go out again in the spring. Trays and trays of tiny plants emerged from his bench.

'What's that one?' she asked almost idly.

'This is borage, a special mountain borage. It seldom survives transplanting.'

'How do we come to have it?'

'Your great-grandmother brought it to the house. She used to overwinter it on the fell. She would have the plants taken up just before Christmas and brought down in the spring.'

'Do you still do that?'

'I take one or two up each year, just to make sure. We refrigerate the rest. I'm just dividing and re-bedding them. They will go back outside in April.'

'How often do you have to do that?' Flora asked.

'Every year.'

'It's been done every year since my great-grandmother brought them?'

'Reckon so. But it was "it" at first not "them". At first there was only one.'

As he spoke, he continued to work and Flora continued to eat her cake. They were both at peace, moving unhurriedly and ritualistically.

'I remember climbing up to the top with my father. By then there were two trays. He used to call it "Julia traipsing". He remembered going up with Julia herself between the wars. He told me that she always wore trousers and walked with a limp and that she told him, as they climbed, how she came to lose her leg after falling from a crag whilst gathering the borage. That was why she took so much trouble with it.'

'My great-grandmother only had one leg?'

'Yes.'

'Are there other plants here that she brought?'

'Most of these I shouldn't wonder. My father said that she was a remarkable woman. She travelled a lot, even after the leg, mostly in Europe.'

'Are you telling me this because of this?' Flora asked, tapping the arm of her chair.

'I'm telling you because you asked me.'

'What do you think about me and David?'

Matt grinned, stopped working, and turned to give her his full attention.

'So there is a "you and David" is there?'

'You know there is!'

113

'I've hoped that you might get together for many a year,' he said. 'Ever since you were little children I hoped that this might happen.'

'Will it work, Matt?'

'Do you doubt it?'

'Not really, except it would be wrong to tie David down, wouldn't it? He needs his freedom. He needs to be out in the world, not shackled by the estate.'

'That's true,' Matt agreed. 'But he need not be chained by the garden. He has the learning to rise above it.'

'It's not just that,' Flora whispered.

'You mean this?' and now he tapped the arm of her chair.

She nodded.

'That's up to you,' he said.

'Oh, not you as well!' Flora snapped. 'I know what they say, but I really can't walk, you know.'

'That's not what I meant, lass,' Matt said gently. 'I know that you would get out of the chair if you could. What I meant is that it's up to you what you make of it. It can mean as little or as much as you want.'

'I need to be free too, Matt. Is that wrong?'

'That depends.'

'On what?'

'On what you mean to do with it. You're both very young. Falling in love is not the end, it's the beginning. Long-term love is not looking at each other all the time, it's looking at the world together.'

'But what am I to do with myself?'

'What about your painting? You talk about painting as though it matters but you just dabble at it, you know. You could be more than an amateur dauber, but that's up to you. You have to choose.'

'That seems to be your answer to everything. ''It's up to you!'' '

114

'That's right. It always is.'

Flora considered for a while and then said, 'I'm really happy, Matt.'

'I know that, flower, and I'm really happy for you.'

Matt went back to his bench and expertly turned a pot up, removing the plant without damage. Flora put the last of the marzipan in her mouth. She felt warm and happy.

'How do you know what to do, Matt?' she asked. 'You're always busy. How do you know what needs doing?'

'I seem to have always known.'

Flora looked at the silvery leaves.

'Not much to lose a leg for,' she said.

'Nor to spend sixty-five thousand days on.'

'Sixty-five thousand days?'

'Well, not just on this one plant, but I'm the sixth generation of Bennetts to tend this garden.'

'Almost as long as us.'

'One hundred and eighty years at say 350 days a year,' he continued. 'We've given near enough sixty-five thousand days and that's not counting the times when more than one of us was working here. Caffelmeade was once *gafael maed*. It means a field mown in lieu of rent. Appropriate for us Bennetts and Wolsingtons.'

It was as though a camera shutter clicked and then once again I saw Flora as she went into the greenhouse and I knew that it was the next morning. I knew also that Flora was no longer happy. I looked in through the glass and saw that all the pots in the greenhouse were overturned. The only word that I can find to describe what I sensed then is malevolence.

'It looks as though someone has stamped on them,' Flora said forlornly.

Matt said nothing, but brought a broom and began

to sweep the floor. When it was cleared, he locked the door and put the key under a plantpot.

'That's that,' he said.

I shuddered and felt my ankle turn. A plant pot with yet another aspidistra crashed to the floor. Heather's mother got up from the sewing machine and came to me.

'Are you all right? I thought you were going to stand behind that clothes rack for ever.'

'I'm sorry,' I said.

Mrs Hindle looked at me carefully.

'Hey, it doesn't matter, you know. It's not the biggest aspidistra in the world! Don't take everything so seriously! It was an accident, wasn't it?'

12

Silver birches now stand in English gardens like the ghosts of Mother Russia.

Philip stood with me before the pictures. I could tell that he was feeling silly and was probably sorry that he had come with me. I had told him again about my trips to Caffelmeade, this time telling him what had happened in some detail. At first he had laughed.

'Nice try, Annie. Pull the other leg!'

Then when he realized that I was serious he said, 'But you've just been daydreaming! I bet that everything in your garden is wonderful. This Flora is just like you, isn't she? And David's your ideal boyfriend? Everyone does it, you know!'

He had grown more interested when I told him that everything was far from well in the garden, and that I had also been with other people in other times. He had asked questions and I had answered truthfully. Then he said, 'Well, it does seem a bit weird.'

'If it's a hyperstring, Philip, then you were right, it is instantaneous.'

Philip laughed. 'But you do know that we were only knocking a few ideas about, don't you? I mean, there's no such thing as a hyperstring.' Then he added, 'And even if there was, the chances of you getting tangled up like this is one in, oh, I don't know, one in millions of billions.'

'You mean you were just making it up?'

117

'Not exactly. This is different. You must see that!'

'How is it different?'

'We're not making something up that we know to be untrue. We're following a proposition through. We don't step out of the rules.'

'What rules?'

'Rules of science.'

'And one of those rules is public proof, isn't it?'

He nodded.

'Then come with me. Come to the gallery and see what happens.'

He shook his head.

'You're frightened!' I challenged. 'You've not got the courage of your own convictions.'

'I'm not frightened, because nothing will happen.'

'But what if it does?'

And so we were standing looking at the pictures and sure enough nothing happened.

'What did you expect?' he asked.

'I thought that I might find myself inside the garden again. I thought that you might even be drawn through with me, or if not, you could at least tell me if you saw anything.'

'Saw anything?'

'Well, saw a change in me, or something.'

'Perhaps we should hold hands just in case,' Philip said.

'Why, if nothing is going to happen?'

'I didn't say it wouldn't. I said "probably".'

Philip took my hand.

'You're shaking!'

'I half want it to happen to prove that it's possible and half afraid that it will,' he said.

I brought my other hand round and held on to the sleeve of his red shirt.

He looked at the painting more closely.

'It's not very good, is it?'

'Isn't it?'

'No. I mean it's a bit unclear. Even after two goes at it it's not very definite, is it?' He pointed to Rosie. 'Look at the kid's kim—'

I saw a flash of brilliant red away beyond the silver birches. It was cold in the wood, papery white bark against the snow, black branches tracing a milky sky. It was winter and must have been before her fall for Flora trudged along the path. She was wearing jeans, boots, a padded coat, and ear muffs. In her hands she carried large bunches of holly. She stopped as though listening for something and then trudged on. Once again she stopped and this time she spun on her heel as though trying to catch someone by surprise. Again I saw the flash of red through the birches. This time it was closer.

'Stop messing about!' Flora called.

No answer.

'Come on, David,' she shouted. 'It's not funny.'

No answer.

She walked on, glancing about her as she went.

A glimpse of red. She had seen it too. She turned and started to walk back. I found that I was walking close by her. She was frightened. The wood was quiet. No birds. No crackles. Nothing but the sound of Flora's breathing. Not true. There was another breathing quite close by. As we walked and then ran a little and then slowed down again, so too did the other.

Flora gasped and recoiled and I looked down at a dead badger. It was lying on its back with stiff snout and paws in the air. There was no blood. Further on we found dead birds lying as though they had just fallen from the air. Flora lost her footing and put her hand down. She stayed still as though frozen and stared at her hand. I looked and saw that she had put her hand on a rabbit. I knew that it was still warm, but I also knew that it was quite dead.

She looked up, straight at me and our eyes should have met, but she was focused beyond me, almost, as it were, through me. I turned and then I stared too. Behind me was a silver birch, the trunk straight and slim and white against the winter darkness of the rhododendrons, the light silhouette turning dark where it thrust free of the shrubs and showed against the sky. It was a tree like any other except that an ass's head leered down from its branches. It fell, tearing through the twigs to settle again nearer to us. It seemed to wink.

Then we ran, Flora scattering holly berries on the white floor. Now the breathing was ahead of us. We stopped. Flora was uncertain which way to go and she began to sob.

'—ono, it's not even properly finished. You can't see where it ends and the background begins,' Philip said, then, 'What's the matter, Annie?'

'Were you in the birch wood?' I asked.

'Was I where?'

'I've just been in the birch wood at Caffelmeade. Flora was frightened by someone. I thought that it might be you.'

'What are you going on about?'

'I tell you I've just been there,' and I stabbed my finger at the wood in the background of the painting.

'No you haven't,' he said. 'You've been here all the time so that proves it.'

'Proves what?'

'That you just imagine it.'

'No. It just shows us that you can't come with me and that no one can tell when it happens.'

'This is nuts!'

'Just one more question?'

He looked resigned.

'Would a person sucked along a hyperstring be in any danger?'

'Mr Smithers told you. They'd be dead.'

'But suppose they weren't? Suppose they could slip back and forth, then would they really be in the other place. I mean could they be hurt? Could they die there?'

'Oh! Annie,' he shook his head, 'how do I know? I wish I'd never said anything about it!'

'Look, just there,' I said. 'I've never noticed that speck of scarlet in the wood before. What do you think it's meant to be?'

'I don't know and neither do you. And don't you go making anything up.'

He saw that I was trying not to cry. 'Look, Annie, Caffelmeade's a real place and these were real people. Why don't you find out about them and stop day-dreaming? And for goodness' sake stop thinking about hyperstrings. You don't understand!'

That was true. I did not understand, but then neither did he. I was not ready to let it go then because it was still the most reasonable explanation I had. It was, after all, the only one that did not point to me.

13

In 1828 two seeds of the giant waterlily, Victoria amazonica, *were brought from South America packed in wet clay but although they germinated they produced no flowers. Twenty years later one bloomed at Chatsworth. Sixty years after this a postcard was for sale showing a small child sitting on a leaf which bore its weight above the water.*

The rehearsal was a mess. It was as though we had forgotten everything that we had learned. The comic subplot was a humour-free zone, while the lovers raised sniggers. Peaseblossom fell off her swing because the loose-fitting sweetpea bonnet fell over her eyes, and Cobweb, after climbing the rope successfully trailing behind him the long glittering strings of his web, then ran out of gossamer threads and could not get down. Puck forgot his lines, even the ones he had known from the very beginning and Philip, well, Philip had gone back to mumbling. I knew that all was well though. I knew because of so many little signs, the way he took my hand even when not strictly necessary, the way he looked at me when he thought I could not see him.

'Don't worry,' Miss Ogle said when we had finished. 'This often happens. It *will* be all right on the night. The bus'll be here in half an hour. The scene painters and the lighting people please have a word with me now. Enjoy the play tonight and we'll meet next Thursday for the dress rehearsal.'

The stage began to empty from the back. As the principals waited to get to the steps Heather put her hand on Sam's back and he turned to her and they began to talk quietly to each other.

'He'll need a bit of encouragement,' the old lady had said. I turned to Philip with a smile. He was already talking to 'Titania'.

'Are you and Annice together now?' I heard Elspeth ask.

'No,' Philip answered.

'Are you sure?' she persisted coyly.

'Of course I am.'

'I thought that you might like the arty kind.'

'I like the long-haired blonde kind. Anyway, she isn't artistic.'

'Isn't she?'

'No. She's just dippy.'

Isolated between the two couples, I felt sick.

'Thank your father for the drawings, Annie,' Miss Ogle called. 'I'm sure that we can use some of the ideas. When is your cousin coming? If she could see the dress rehearsal I'm sure that she could give us some tips.'

'Oh, I forgot!' I stammered. 'She's not able to come after all.'

'That's a pity! I was looking forward to meeting her. Do you suppose that she might come if I wrote to her? A formal invitation?'

'No!' I almost shouted. 'She's . . . she's . . . going for an audition.'

'Something interesting?'

'Just a commercial.'

'I see.'

Miss Ogle walked further off down the hall and scanned the stage. I blew on my upper lip. I would never, never, make up a story again. Never again.

'It looks bare,' Miss Ogle said. 'Even with the extra gauzes it will look stark. We could do with some flowers or plants to stand in front of the stage.'

'I could bring you some aspidistras,' Heather offered.

'And I could bring some flowers from our hothouses,' I added. 'They're full.'

I turned away so that nobody would see my face. 'Never' had lasted less than a minute.

'Thank you both.'

In the cloakroom I looked in the mirror. I no longer looked radiant as I had in the morning, now I looked shiny, the severe hair style no longer sophisticated, just plain, the dress no longer simple, just dowdy. I knew then what I had always suspected, that I was not the stuff of fairytales. Quickly, before I could begin to cry, I shrugged the dress off and pulled on my embroidered jeans, my painted T-shirt, and the sweater of a hundred yarns that had taken my mother months to knit. I removed the hairband and let my hair tumble. On Monday, I promised myself, I would get a new hair dye. I picked up the rucksack and began to stuff the dress in and then thought better of it and thrust it into the waste bin, spitefully pushing it right down amongst the Coke cans and the crisp packets.

On the bus I found myself sitting next to 'Oberon' who was already deep into an aircraft magazine. I looked fixedly out of the window as we drove through the industrial heart of the city past steel works, railway sheds, and old cotton warehouses, and then through the city centre. I closed my eyes as we passed the end of our street and opened them when I knew that the bus had reached the river.

We went over the bridge that put us into Salford and I looked downriver to the new developments, the town houses and flats, the hotels and the riverside pubs strung with coloured lights. Next past the prison with its bricked cliff walls and the minaret rising above the sprawl of discount shops. Then houses, getting newer and bigger, as they got further from the city centre. Then we were passing through town villages with shopping centres and the street became an avenue and then a road and finally a motorway and we were in the country. Now we were passing farms. Across the fields I could see a large house showing itself in glimpses through trees so dense that lights were already burning in the windows. It would be warm inside.

The fire burned fiercely in the iron grate and Flora stood before an easel. I looked closely at her. She was a little older, maybe nineteen? Twenty? It was quite definitely after the accident but she was walking, or rather standing.

We were in the great hall and it was a mess. There was a jumble of masonry under the Jacobean cupboards, a broken bit of column from the old folly, a stone pineapple from the gatepost, a Corinthian capital from an old façade. There was an assortment of shabby dolls, sheep's skulls, stuffed lion's heads, and horns scattered about. A nasty modern carpet was laid across the stone flags and no one had managed to hoover it. The great oak table was clear, however, and well polished and it softly reflected the swords, spears, and rifles arranged in a fan on the wall above it.

A cat walked towards me along the carpet strip followed by its trail of kittens. It was grey like Grisaille but I knew, as I knew everything, that it was called Smoke. It rubbed itself around my legs, leaving a ring of hairs in the denim.

The kittens had begun to explore, climbing the legs of the chairs, catching at the lower edges of the tapestries with their pin-like claws, attaching themselves to the calf of Flora's jeans. A grey tabby kitten had climbed the easel and a calico kitten had scampered through the palette which Flora had set down and now left smudgy paw-prints of ochre, and cobalt, and crimson on the floor.

Flora was painting the heavy heads of winter aconite, and achingly tender shoots of snowdrops.

It's cruel, I thought, things will keep growing. The garden is remorseless.

'What did you say?'

'Nothing, I was dreaming.'

Another page of the flying magazine was turned and I went back to gazing from the bus window. I felt ill. I had not enjoyed my daydream. My imagined people, for at that moment that is what I thought they were, used to be friends, friends who never let me down and who came when bidden. Now they came unwanted. Caffelmeade was a slovenly neglected mess. I looked across at Philip who was smiling foolishly at 'Titania'. Everything was spoiled.

The audience had seated themselves as directed by the stewards. Some were perched on the grassy hillside, some had come equipped with camping stools and had placed them at the edge of a sandy area, still others had brought tables and all the paraphernalia of a proper picnic and had obviously had their evening meal there. The play was to open in a natural amphitheatre created by a hollow in the ground and surrounded by the fantastic shapes of weathered sandstone rocks.

I looked around uncertain where to sit. Philip had settled with his back to a rock and 'Titania' slid down beside him. Heather and Sam had spread their coats on the grass and were being joined by Miss Ogle. I felt desolate. One minute I was coping, the next I was plunged into despair, as inconsolable as only those who build their lives on lies can be.

'Come and sit with us,' Heather called to me.

I made my way over the bodies and had just settled myself beside them when 'Theseus' peeled himself from a rock and stepped into the arena. The front of his costume was brilliant but the back was the colour of sandstone so that he could melt away by turning to the cliff.

> *'Now, fair Hippolyta, our nuptial hour*
> *Draws on apace;'*

As he spoke he stretched out his hand towards one of the weathered stacks and a hand joined his and Hippolyta was revealed. At the same time, at the other side of the circle Philostrate turned chameleon-like from his camouflaged position.

The play began. It was a promenade performance and we had to follow the players as they roamed through the wood. The audience was a nuisance. I would have liked to stalk the play by myself, hiding behind trees to overhear the lovers, stealthily creeping to the edge of the old quarry where the fairies swung on trapezes and ropes, sitting quietly by the stream as the mechanicals rehearsed their play. This was not possible because however hard the stewards worked it was difficult moving so many people about. Some of the audience were ill-prepared and we had to wait for stiletto heels to be dug out of the ground, and for the arrival of the picnic baskets, the travel rugs, and the collapsible chairs. The actors had no lighting to signal the start and relied on the attentive audience to shush the gossips. Even so, the magic of the play soon took over.

When Bottom reappeared after being 'translated' he was an ass from the front and the weaver from behind, his costume of motley front and brown back reversed. Titania, asleep in a nest of blossoms bivouacked halfway up a rock, awoke to find him climbing down towards her.

'*What angel wakes me from my flowery bed?*'

I saw Flora wake and knew that it was her birthday. Flora plumped up her pillows and reached to the bedside table for a photograph. She smiled the strangest of smiles. This, I knew, was a time of enchantment for Flora.

Elizabeth and Rosie came into the room and sat on Flora's bed.

'I'm so glad that you're having a proper party, darling,' Elizabeth said. 'We need something to cheer us up.' She said no more. Nobody referred directly to Flora's fall nor to the damage in the garden. This was the nearest they came to it. The same superstition possessed them all. It had not happened if they did not name it.

'Matt should be bringing the flowers soon,' Elizabeth continued. 'I'll deal with them. The men should come to finish the marquee about eleven. The caterers should arrive at five, the musicians at seven thirty. The guests arrive from seven. Dinner is at eight. Let's hope the weather holds, because marquees can be very draughty. The dancing will start about nine thirty.'

I don't want to be here, I thought. I do not want to be here. I want to watch the play. I squeezed my eyes shut and after a while opened them again.

'When do we dress up?' Rosie demanded bouncing up and down on the bed.

'As soon as you like,' Elizabeth answered.

'The dance will be lovely,' Rosie said keeping the bounce vigorous.

'You'll be too tired to come to the dance,' Flora told her, 'and stop jiggling about!'

'Shall!' Rosie said stubbornly, bouncing some more.

'She can't,' Flora appealed to her mother, 'she simply can't spoil the dancing. She'll rush about under their feet, or David will have to pretend to waltz with her.'

'You won't even see me,' Rosie protested. 'You'll only see David.' And Rosie widened her eyes and rolled them round and round and then put her finger down her throat and made sick-making noises.

'It'll be all right,' Elizabeth said, but it was not obvious to which daughter she spoke. They both appeared satisfied.

'Are you coming for a drink?'

'Annie! Are you coming for a drink?'

I looked about me and realized that the actors were walking away, the play had stopped.

'Where've you been?' Heather joked. 'Away with the fairies?' She peered at me and then said, 'I suppose you must have seen it done better?'

'It's fine,' I said. Then I saw that Heather was disappointed. 'Not as good as the RSC, of course,' I added, and Heather smiled.

'I thought that you must have seen better,' she said. 'Who have you seen in it?'

I hesitated, trying to remember what I had said about it before. Had I claimed to have seen it before? I was getting muddled; no longer sure which bits of my imagined life I had told.

'Leave her be,' Sam said. 'We'll bring her a drink. She looks tired out.'

I am, I thought. This is very tiring. I have to be constantly on my guard, constantly scanning, constantly running a scenario in my head. I am tired.

'Flowers,' Matt said unnecessarily as he came through

129

the kitchen door, his arms full of greenery and the occasional rose. 'This must be the worst time of year for flowers that can be cut. It's too late and too soon.'

'It's what?'

'Too late for the bulbs, for daffodils and tulips, and too soon for most of the roses and the herbaceous.'

'Sorry. I should have thought of that sixteen years ago,' Elizabeth said drily.

'Are you in costume?' she asked.

'This is what you get,' Matt replied. 'I'm a parson gardener from the eighteenth century. No one in particular. Just a type.'

'I see. I'm Great-Grandmother Julia,' and Elizabeth's hand went to the cameo at her throat.

He looked down, and Elizabeth laughed, 'Oh, before the fall! I'm not hopping on one leg all day!'

'Flora is doing something with a net curtain!'

David came into the room.

'Will you close your eyes, please? Yum Yum wishes to make her entrance.'

Elizabeth and Matt made a pretence of closing their eyes, elaborately covering them with their hands. Into the room came Rosie in her kimono, taking tiny little steps and fluttering her fan in front of her face.

'Why!' Matt said, bringing his hands down. 'Will you introduce me?'

'It's me!' Rosie squealed. 'Look, Matt. It's me!'

'Will you come outside for a moment?' David asked.

I followed them with reluctance. Flora had set a camera on a tripod facing the house and they grouped themselves together. Flora spread her curtain-net dress wide to cover the wheels of the chair and held the remote shutter release on her lap. I went to the camera and looked through the viewfinder although I knew only too well what I would see.

'Come on, Annie, we're on the move again!' Heather almost shouted.

I scrambled to my feet and, clutching my rucksack and my jacket, tagged along. This is hopeless, I said to myself, I can't concentrate for more than two lines before the others take over. Get out of my head! Get out of my head! I chanted to myself, as we trooped after the guide, who led us now across the sloping lawns.

'You could have brought Rosie,' Heather said. 'There's lots of kids and Miss Ogle wouldn't have minded.'

'Rosie?'

'I wish I had a sister.'

The scene of the mechanicals' performance of *Pyramus and Thisbe* was to take place in a long, narrow, wooded hollow. Logs had been wedged up the steep banks to make seating but they were already full and so Heather, Sam, and I perched uncomfortably on the ground, wedging our feet as best we could. Philip and 'Titania' came even later and I wondered if they had lingered in some dell. 'Titania' looked languidly along the log seating and the people rose and made a place for her.

'Hm!' Heather said and then smiled wryly.

Philip came and perched near us.

' 'Tis strange, my Theseus, that these lovers speak of.'

The birthday was over, the last couples calling their farewells. The musicians were packing their instruments, folding their music stands and shrugging on their coats. Rosie lay in a crumpled sleepy heap under one of the tables. Only the keyboard player still played, improvising around a melody, making it at once familiar and strange.

'May I have this dance?' David asked and before Flora could reply he had picked her up in his arms and started to move to the music of the lone pianist.

131

'I have something for you,' David said when the music finally stopped. He placed her carefully back in her chair. 'I have to bring it from the car. Will you wait for me?'

Don't say 'For ever' I silently pleaded but too late.

'For ever,' Flora said.

Rosie was wakened by the silence and sat up rubbing her eyes. David returned carrying a cellophane box.

'It's a Wolsington China Pink!' Flora exclaimed.

'It's the rose that your mother dropped.'

'But how . . .?'

'Not quite as poetic as pressing it, I'm afraid, but the result is better. I microwaved it.'

Rosie got to her feet.

'Flora!' she called, but Flora was not in the mood to hear her. She went to David and pulled gently at his trouser leg.

'Not now, Rosie,' he muttered.

She pulled at her sister's sleeve.

'Flora!'

Flora shook her arm gently as though dislodging a puppy or a kitten.

'Go away, Rosie,' she whispered.

Rosie's lips trembled. She felt shut out. She used to be David's girl. He used to say, 'Where's my girl?' But she did not cry, she stumped out of the marquee, thumping her feet noisily. I followed her to the gate where she tried to attract her mother's attention. Elizabeth was seeing the guests out through the garden gate, exchanging farewells. I was only mildly surprised to see that one of them looked like Heather's grandmother. She was wearing a glamorous satin dress the exact colour of her pyjamas.

'Just go to bed, Rosie,' Elizabeth said.

'Come with me.'

'Be a big girl now. Go up on your own. I'll come later.'

Rosie trailed away dragging her feet, the picture of utter dejection. Then she began to mutter incantations against her neglect.

'I hope that Flora never has another strawberry,' she said, for strawberries were her latest delight. 'I hope that David's car won't start and that he has to walk home. And I hope that it rains on him.' She went on making up worse and worse curses because there was something comforting about being so forlorn, like the envy that she felt of orphans in stories. Forgotten now were the tiny steps of the geisha as she made long, weary, melodramatic strides. She would not go to bed. She would hide. Then they would look for her, and they would worry. They would run all over looking for her and they might think that she had run away or that she was dead. Then they would be sorry.

No! I wanted to shout.

I did shout, but of course Rosie could not hear me.

'Wake up, Annie,' Heather nudged me.

I sat bolt upright and opened my eyes very wide. I started to push my nails into my palms so that the pain would keep me awake.

> *'O grim-look'd night! O night with hue so black!*
> *O night, whichever art when day is not!'*

Rosie went to the stove house. It was very hot. The sprinklers were playing, the water turning constantly to steam. The leaves of the big water-lily were almost open. She took off the belt with the bolster and let her kimono fall open. She started to undo her shoes and then thought that the leaf might feel funny on her feet, so left them laced up. The lily pad didn't look as big as in the photograph she had seen and she hesitated, but only

133

for a moment. She stood on the edge of the pool and then stepped on to the immature leaf of the *Victoria amazonica*.

The leaf did not bear her up, even for a moment. She slid into the water as surely as if she had stepped straight into a swimming pool. She did not panic at first for she could swim and the pool was only four feet deep. As soon as her shoes touched the bottom she pushed up strongly. She broke through the surface of the water but underneath a leaf, as thick and elastic as a sheet of rubber. She was catapulted back to the bottom. Still she did not panic. She came up again and was once more thrust back.

Each time she came up she gulped for the limited air that got under or through the leaves, but now it hurt and she began to thrash without thought. Each time now she stayed under longer and fought her way up with more trouble. She was too weak to hold the leaves clear of the surface whilst keeping herself afloat. Her shoes filled with water and the leather swelled making them tighter and heavier than ever. Suddenly she felt all right. She felt warm and comfortable. She stopped struggling. The *Victoria amazonica* settled back serenely on the still water.

'Oh no!' I moaned and felt myself slip. I would have slid down the bank and been catapulted into the action of the play had not Philip caught me and held me until I regained my footing.

'Are you all right?' Heather mouthed silently.

I nodded bleakly knowing that I was not all right, I was very far from being all right. It had been fun rummaging through literature, extracting people and events for my make-believe world, and until now it had done no harm. It was a harmless pastime, I had always told myself, almost a hobby that I could pick up anywhere, anytime, to fill in a lonely minute or even an hour. It was all right, I told myself, to pretend that the family at Caffelmeade were my real family but really silly to tell others that they were. Now the game was no longer amusing or even comforting. Why had I killed Rosie? What harm had Rosie ever done?

The scream was prolonged and purposeful, theatrical and unreal. Philip's grip tightened on my arm as the audience looked up the hillside towards the noise, expecting the arrival of Bottom. We could see nothing. The actors had stopped, falling out of character, and also looking towards the screech, searching the gloom. Unease swept through the audience like a Mexican wave.

'Oh no!' Miss Ogle whispered and was surprised when everyone turned towards her. 'It's our Puck. He's fallen.'

A light was swivelled and the small body disclosed where it lay at the foot of the grotesquely weathered sandstone.

14

The plant is sometimes called dittany but more commonly the 'burning bush' because on hot days when the seed pods are ripe they give off a volatile gas which can be ignited by a match.

I sat quite still as people ran to the rock. They formed a circle leaving me outside. I watched as the backs of the crowd parted to admit two people with the white bandoliers of the St John's Ambulance Brigade. One was an incredibly old man the other a little boy of about ten. I could not move. I closed my eyes.

The people stood in a circle outside the conservatory in their fancy dress. Columbines drooped, Napoleons held back tears, gladiators let their shoulders fall and St George's sword lay in the dust.

I was inside. The moonlight picked out the curling edges of the glossy leaves of the giant water-lily. I saw Rosie's belt with its tiny bolster and then, in the corner of my eyes, a wisp of pink in the pool. I could not move. I could not even turn my head to confront the slither of fabric that I knew without any doubt was the kimono.

'Rosie!' David shouted as he jumped into the pool and caught hold of the silk. He hauled the body of the little girl up, dragging the huge flat sheets of leaves with her. He tore them away ferociously and lifted her clear. He laid her down and began the slow, methodical

136

business of breathing for her, although he knew it was too late.

The circle of backs parted and I saw Philip and Sam pick up the fallen Puck and start towards the carpark. The blancoed belts of St John stood out starkly. I still did not move.

It was morning at Caffelmeade and the men were dismantling the marquee. They did it alone. No one was able to help them. Matt was sitting on the seat under the tree rhododendrons. It was a good place to sit beneath the smooth, silky red bark, and the explosion of glossy leaves. Elizabeth came and sat quietly beside him. He could think of nothing to say to her. What does one say to a mother the day after her child was drowned?

'They look so wrong here, in an English garden,' she said.

'Perhaps they shouldn't be in an English garden,' Matt replied. 'Rousseau said that nature shuns frequented places. We have forced plants to come and live with us and done them some violence on the way. That is what gives them an element of unreality.'

'Rousseau said that?'

'Well. Something like it. I think that we should let it go, Elizabeth.'

'What do you mean?'

'I think that we should let nature in. Let the garden grow how it will. When the roses burned I felt angry but I was also relieved. The garden is destroying itself and I'm free to go.'

'Where?'

'Who knows? First I'm going to China. I'm going to take this little tree home.'

He tapped a polythene bag with his foot and Elizabeth saw a young sapling.

'The handkerchief tree?'

He nodded and got to his feet. Elizabeth stood with him.

'When will you go?'

'Soon.'

'Come along, Annie,' Miss Ogle said briskly. 'We're going.'

I followed her. It was dark now and at first we had to walk single file along a rabbit track and even when we joined the path we had to watch our footing on the loose stones.

'It's a shame to miss the last act,' Miss Ogle said. 'We'll have to find another Puck and that will be almost impossible at this late date. I might have to read it. Might your folks be able to help?'

I tried to understand. I tried telling myself that shock affects people in strange ways. I tried telling myself that 'the show must go on'. I tried all kinds of mind tricks to explain Miss Ogle's callous reaction to the little boy's death, but I could not.

'But will the play go on?' I mumbled.

'Of course,' Miss Ogle said cheerily. 'It'll take more than the tricks of that little monkey to stop it.'

I stood quite still.

Miss Ogle stopped too. 'What's the matter with you, Annice?'

Then I saw Miss Ogle's face crease and twitch and I realized that she was laughing. She was actually laughing. A child falls to his death and his teacher laughs. The world is gone mad.

'I know we say "break a leg" but we don't expect to be taken quite so literally,' Miss Ogle spluttered. 'I'm sorry, I shouldn't laugh, he's probably in pain, but remember that wonderful scream! A ham to the end! You've got to admire him.'

Puck was not dead. It was Rosie who was dead.

'He's broken his leg?' I asked.

'Not him,' Miss Ogle replied. 'But it's a bad enough sprain. He can't go swinging about on ropes. Come on, let's be a bit quicker. They're waiting for us. I'm looking forward to meeting your parents next week and thanking your father.'

Parents' evening! I had forgotten! But there was an easy way to keep them away from school. I would simply not tell them about it. I would have to think of an excuse to explain their absence, of course.

'I'm not sure that they'll be able to come . . .' I began.

'Yes they are,' Miss Ogle told me cheerfully. 'They've already sent the reply slip back.'

'You post them?'

'Yes. We've found it best. Those that have something to hide sometimes just "forget" to take the invitations home.'

I hauled myself on to the bus thinking furiously of a way to prevent my parents from meeting my teachers, because if they did, I would be found out. 'Oberon' was still deep in his magazine and stood to let me get past him without taking his eyes from the page. I rested my head against the trembling window. There was nothing much to see except isolated lights glimmering feebly.

It was dim in the room although Flora had switched on all the lights. The wooden panelling and the high ceilings seemed to soak it up. She stood in a bright spotlight created by two great anglepoise lamps. She stood close up to her easel painting quickly, her brush darting from the canvas to the palette where it swirled and scrubbed in the paint and then flashing back to the painting where it jabbed repeatedly like a kingfisher flirting with the river.

She was out of the wheelchair.

She was absorbed. I went to stand behind her knowing what I would see, and sure enough, the familiar first painting of 'The Birthday Party' was emerging. The fancy dress that they had worn was lying about the room. Matt's black, Elizabeth's corset, the piece of lace that Flora herself had worn, David's vivid blue cravat. A photograph was pinned to the corner of the canvas. Flora was not looking at any of them, she painted from some memory more accurate than they could ever be. Most of the figures were simply charcoal outlines, but Flora had almost finished Rosie. She rocked back on her heels and then the brush went forward again, but this time slowly and with tenderness. A smiling Rosie now looked out from the canvas.

'Annie,' Miss Ogle said, swaying in the aisle of the bus. 'The flowers, Annie. You will be able to get the flowers, won't you? You promised to bring them from your garden?'

My heart shrank as I remembered and I felt my skin turn pale and then red.

'Do you feel unwell?' Miss Ogle asked. 'We'll be stopping at the motorway service station. Will you be all right until then?'

I nodded.

I went straight to the toilets at the service station and hid in a cubicle. I expected someone to come to look for me, waited for Heather or Miss Ogle to call my name. Nobody came.

I had been thinking too long about the thoughts in my head, about the garden and the people at Caffelmeade, about the possibilities. Maybe Miss Ogle was right and I had just got indigestion from reading too much without

140

chewing it. I did not really believe this. Maybe Philip's notion of hyperstrings was right and I was being boomeranged back and forth between times and places. It seemed so unlikely, but so did men walking on the moon and silly little supermarket trolleys trundling across Mars. I wanted to believe in this, and I had kidded myself that I did for a time, because then I would not be to blame. I could not believe it, of course. Not even Philip believed it. I was left with the thought that it was my own fantasy and the knowledge that it had got out of control. I think that at that moment I truly thought that I was losing my mind.

I slid down to the ground and put my hands in my pockets. My fingers found stiff paper and I took out the bits of the postcard. Idly I pieced it together on the mock mosaic of the lavatory floor. It lay, a fragmented world, with its torn edges showing white.

People are as well as the stories that they tell themselves. Healthy people tell themselves healthy stories. I knew myself to be sickening by the strange happenings at Caffelmeade.

They stood in front of the beehives. 'We must tell the bees,' Flora had said. 'Matt told Rosie that if the bees weren't told the important things then they would swarm away. He said that we must always talk to the bees. She believed him and always told them our news.'

Elizabeth stepped forward and licked her lips.

'Bees, you know what has happened here. Rosie will not come to talk to you again.'

I saw the little group as though from above and noticed that Elizabeth Wolsington's hair was quite a glowing red, almost like my mother's.

'Bees,' Matt said, and I looked at him and saw him run his hands through his hair with my father's familiar gesture, 'I am going. I'm sure that you knew that before I did. The garden is going to change. It has grown old. It must be renewed.'

'I'm going to look after Caffelmeade. I'll do my best and I hope that you will stay with us,' David said. There was something familiar about the set of David's shoulders, something about the way his hair parted and I realized that he was more like Philip than he was like the boy in the painting.

I looked at Flora and was relieved. At least she was not like anyone I knew. Certainly not me. As I was thinking this, Flora slowly got up out of her wheelchair and walked unsteadily forward.

'As you see, bees, I can walk,' was all she said.

I picked up the pieces of the postcard to put them into my book for safe keeping. In my mind I heard Philip saying, 'It's a real place, you know. Caffelmeade really exists.'

I turned the fragments over. At some time Philip had written on the back:

'NB—check pattern of the maze'

There, printed at the bottom, were the words, 'Caffelmeade. Alnwick. Northumberland. Home of the Wolsington Family.'

I went out on to the forecourt and the bus had gone. I had no clear idea of what I was going to do. Maybe I would telephone home and get my father to come for me? Maybe I would hitch a lift into town? I had to think. I had to plan. Perhaps I could telephone to Heather in a little while and get someone to come for me and stay at her house? I could say that my family were away. Maybe I could telephone Philip? Maybe he would come for me. I was so very tired. I just wanted everything to stop for a while.

The furniture removals van travelled at exactly fifty miles

an hour, steadily eating up the twisted ribbon of the road. We were on the top of the Pennines, nothing beside us but dispirited bracken and dirty heather under a grid of drystone walls, and nothing above but grey emptiness, curlews, and lapwings. The lorry wound up and down and back and forth like a sidewinder snake.

'The rolling English drunkard,' the driver began and I joined in, 'Made the rolling English road.'

'It's not true, you know,' he added. 'Most of the roads were made by Irishmen, but it's a pity to spoil a good rhyme.'

I relaxed a bit. I had gone down the lines of lorries in the motorway carpark and chosen the removals van because I reckoned that removals men were trusted, were admitted into homes, were allowed to drive away with precious things. I had a lot of experience of removal men. I had none of hitching lifts. I knew it was stupid. I knew it was dangerous. At that moment I did not care.

When the driver came I was reassured because he was quite old and thin and quietly spoken. Nevertheless I sat on my hands on the edge of my seat as though I could spring out of the cab if I needed to, which was an illusion because he had locked my door.

'Just to the nearest railway station?' I had asked. 'I'm not hitching. I've just got left behind. I can buy a ticket from there.'

He had not tried to talk to me and I was glad of that at first but now I was starting to find the silence threatening. The Chesterton rhyme was the first thing that he had said after, 'I can get you to Leeds.'

'It's bleak up here,' I now offered.

'Aye. Spring's the worst, you know. In the summer it's mauve and in the autumn it's bronze and purple and in the winter it's white. It's only in the spring that it's like this. You're not from round here, then?'

143

'No,' I agreed. 'From Northumberland. I'm from Alnwick.'

'A Geordie? I'd never have guessed from your accent. You'll be getting a train to Newcastle, then?'

Newcastle?

'Yes,' I agreed.

I fancied that we had been dropping down for a while. The road still rose and fell but the overall feeling was down. The roadsides now had the first spiky leaves of the rosebay willowherb. He saw that I was looking at them.

'They're rosebay willowherb, you know,' he told me. 'You'd know them in the summer. They have tall spikes of purple flowers and in the autumn the seeds blow everywhere in clouds. I remember once in Manchester, when they were clearing the old terraced houses, you know, having to put the windscreen wipers on.'

He looked to see that I was listening and then went on.

'They're a weed. They only came to England after the war, you know. Never had trouble with them before that. My dad used to call them Hitler's revenge.'

'That can't be right,' I said, pulling the book from my pocket. 'It says in here that they were in an English garden three hundred years ago.'

He glanced at the book to see if I was pulling his leg but saw that it was about plants right enough.

'That so?' he asked huffily.

'Yes,' I went on seriously, reading to him from the book. 'It is associated with the second world war because the bombing opened up the land and gave the seeds the right habitat to flourish.'

'You're a funny one to be roving about on your own, you know. Did nobody ever tell you that it was dangerous?'

'I can take care of myself,' I challenged, and then before I could stop myself added, 'you know.'

'I doubt that.'

He pulled the van off the road and turned in his seat. I balled my fists, but he said, 'Take it easy! I've done my hours. Coffee? Do you want a drink?'

'I'd like some air.'

'You could wind the window down a bit, you know.' As he said this he leaned across me and I shrank as far back into my seat as I could. I think that he realized that I was frightened and this annoyed him. He flicked the door locks off.

'You could get out for a bit if you want, you know,' he said.

I clambered down from the van and began to walk deliberately slowly on to the moor as though interested in the view and then when I was out of arm's reach I began to quicken my pace.

'I'm only taking five minutes, you know,' he shouted after me.

I began to run, turning to see if he was following me. The driver was still in his cab. He shrugged his shoulders, poured the dregs of his coffee out of the window and switched on the engine.

I ran clumsily through the tussocks, too ignorant of wild plants to keep away from the wet areas until the turf's springiness gave way to the sucking of the bog just inches beneath me and then grey mud oozed up the sides of my shoes. I could see a building but whether it was a house or a barn I could not be sure, but it was somewhere to aim for.

It was dark and I was alone on the moor. The dark was noisy, full of shuffles and skitters, shrieks and whimpers. There were things about me that sighed as they moved but remained shapeless, nameless.

As I got closer to the building I saw that it was a house, an old and shabby house with a For Sale notice swinging from a scaffold. It was like a child's drawing with a central door and four windows evenly placed. It was the basic pattern for all houses. It looked empty.

I banged on the door but with little hope. The woodwork was peeling through five or six layers of slapped-on paint and wires hung loose from where the bell had once been. I had had some idea of telephoning for a taxi to take me into Leeds where there might have been a late train either to Manchester or to Newcastle. I had decided to leave my fate to chance. I would buy a ticket for whichever went first. Manchester or Newcastle.

I went round to the back. I was cold and frightened. The moon was almost full and there were few clouds so that I could see shadows which fed my imagination. I could see animals lying singly or in heaps and supposed that they were sheep, but they could have been anything. Absolute dark would have been friendlier. I was desperate now and looked around for a brick or a large stone, but found none. I took a shoe off and hit the window. It slapped foolishly against the glass. I put it back on and began to search around the house. At last I found a decent sized rock and once more hit the window. It rattled in its frame but did not break. I stood back and threw it. It chipped the window but did not even crack it. I was crying now with frustration as I hurled the rock over and over again at the glass. In the end it broke, a sunburst of cracks, and I wrapped my hand in my sleeve and pushed it in. My sleeve was not very thick and there was some blood but not much.

I hauled myself into the house. The kitchen had stone flags and a deep stone sink set into a cupboard. I turned the tap, and it wheezed and coughed but all that came out was dirt and a dead spider, its legs curled tight.

Nothing, I thought, looked quite so dead as a dead spider. A cheap modern cooker had been left in the fireplace of the original range and a buckled saucepan stood on it, but there was nothing in the cupboards to cook. Although I was sure that the house was empty I moved cautiously. I groped my way up the stairs to the bathroom. It had a small bath, a corner basin narrower than any set of elbows, and a broken lavatory, patched with cement. I could barely see because the windows were so dirty that not even the bright moon could get through and I decided to risk the light switch. Nothing happened.

There were not many choices left. I got into the bath and made a pillow with my bag. I wondered if Miss Ogle had turned the coach round and if they were looking for me. I imagined Miss Ogle fluffing out her feathers and fussing about like a fat hen. Perhaps however they had not noticed at all and everyone had gone contentedly home. That was not such a good thought. When would my parents start to worry and raise a hue and cry? They would surely report me missing but would anyone do anything about it? Perhaps I would become a statistic? Just another runaway.

Some runaway! I could have been at Leeds station now if I had not been so scared and I had even had trouble throwing a brick through a glass window.

Matt came out of the last greenhouse and closed the door gently. It was an unusually hot day and the garden was making a lot of growth. The clergyman was standing by a clump of *Dictamnus* in flower. I knew that Matt had seen him often, but the priest had never responded to him, never spoken to him as he had done to me and to Rosie. Rosie. Rosie. Cosy Rosie posy. The pods of the *Dictamnus* began to pop in the heat and Matt went closer. He had not thought that any were at the

147

point of seeding yet and certainly he could see only the tall flower spikes. The clergyman smiled. Matt took out his lighter and held it over the plant. Soon another pod exploded and the air itself seemed to ignite. Quite quickly he had made a burning bush. The flames crept slowly through the young plants.

Matt walked towards the gates. He looked almost jaunty.

'Don't go!' I heard myself cry. 'Please stay! I'm coming! Wait for me!'

15

*A garden is unnatural. The plants have been forced to
live in places of our choice, not theirs. This introduces
an element of unreality.*

I woke and found myself cold and cramped. The smell
was not of burning plants but of drains and came
from the plughole of the bath. I got stiffly out and
went into a bedroom. The wallpaper was peeling and
turning green. It was a house that would never be dry or
warm. A picture still hung on a nail. It was an embroidery
in cross stitch and said 'Bless this House'. I went to the
window to look out but could see very little. My watch
said two o'clock but I could hardly believe that I had slept
so late. The window sashes were stiff with dirt and paint
but when I got the window open I heard the unmistakable
rumble of a motorway.

I could see now that the house was in a lonely place,
but it was not a quiet place for the motorway sliced
through this wilderness, offering hope of escape but not
the means.

I could see, however, that I was only half a mile or
so above a village and beyond that I thought I could see
the smoky layers of industry. My watch was still going
so it was indeed two in the afternoon not two in the
middle of the night.

I turned out my purse and searched my pockets. I
hoped that there would be enough to get a bus to
Leeds and then a train. I felt bad about the broken

149

window and so drew the greasy curtains to help disguise it.

I walked down to the village. I walked over the scrubby hillside past abandoned cars, horse boxes without wheels, broken farm machinery, and the sheep, the dirty, long-haired, forlorn sheep. Even so early in the afternoon the daylight was already dying of boredom.

In the village I had a bit of luck. The only bus of the day was due within half an hour so I risked spending some money on biscuits and a can of Coke.

As I walked from the bus station to the railway station in Leeds I looked idly in shop windows because such an everyday activity settled my nerves. I could almost convince myself that I was in Manchester on a Saturday afternoon and not embarked upon an enterprise that was starting to seem crazy.

A bank of television sets were all tuned to racing and I amused myself by letting my eyes flow from set to set as the horses ran so that it seemed that they jumped across the screens. Then they were replaced by a newscaster and then shockingly by my parents. My mother and father were being brought to a table spread with a cloth on which microphones stood. There was a woman holding my mother's elbow and a policeman had a guiding hand on my father's shoulder. My mother looked older, her make-up not quite right, her hair somehow sunk, and my father looked small. I could not hear them but I had no need to, I knew that they were making an appeal to me to come home or to my captors to let me go. I stared as a photograph of myself, a school photograph taken two years ago, was put on the screens. I looked around expecting someone to stop and take hold of me, but even the boy in the shop who had been looking my way just smiled. The screens had gone back to racing.

At the station, I jostled my way to a poster which showed the train routes, for I was a bit hazy about Alnwick. Like most people from the south I knew that there were two counties between the Yorkshire border and Scotland but was surprised to see how big they were. I needed to get to Darlington from where trains went to Alnmouth, which looked quite close to Alnwick on the diagram. After buying my ticket I had just ninety pence left. I hoped that I could walk from Alnmouth to Caffelmeade.

I was surprised that the train from Darlington was a big express because I had expected a small two-carriage diesel going into the depths of the country. The train was very full and as I searched for a seat I saw from the booked seat tickets that most of the passengers were going to Edinburgh. I gave in and pulled down the folding seat in the space between the carriages and perched there. When the guard came to check the ticket he looked quizzically at me as though expecting trouble. I fished the ticket out of my rucksack and he studied it very carefully. I thought that he had recognized me.

'Alnmouth?'

'Yes. I'm going to Alnwick.'

I felt shifty and guilty. Slowly he punched the ticket and gave it back to me. After he had gone I went into the toilet cubicle. The mirror was small and starting to craze at the edges but I could see enough to explain the ticket collector's interest. My face was dirty with the remains of tears and blood from my arm, and the purple streaks in my tangled hair glowed under the overhead light. I washed my face and dried it on the paper towels and wished that I was the sort of girl who always carried a make-up bag. I searched my rucksack in vain looking for a comb or a brush but had to make do with running my fingers through my hair and putting my hair band on. I must try to look ordinary, must not draw attention.

Only a handful of people got off the train at Alnmouth and I looked with envy at the cars waiting to meet them. It was dark and I wished that I had not slept so late. I hung back until everyone had gone and then went out on to the road. The signpost said it was two miles into Alnwick and two miles into Alnmouth. There was no bus stop. It was so quiet and deserted that it was difficult to believe that the lighted train had ever been there. I turned towards Alnmouth with the idea of sleeping on the beach and walking or even getting a bus into Alnwick the next morning.

After clearing a housing estate I saw the lights of Alnmouth across the river. It looked more than two miles away but at least I had good shoes and it was not raining. When I got there I found one long street of shops in darkness but strung along it like beads on a necklace were pools of golden light coming from restaurants and hotels. I looked down each side street as I came to it but could not find a way down to the beach. A noisy group of people stood outside a fish and chip shop and I crossed the road to pass on the dark side. I did not want them to see me. I also did not want to go near the fish and chips. The smell twisted my stomach but my money was too precious to spend. I could survive without food until tomorrow and tomorrow I would be at Caffelmeade.

The buildings petered out and then there was a road which doubled back behind the shops. I went along this and found that I had a small golf course on my right and houses to my left. The moon shone fitfully between scudding clouds. Beyond the golf course I imagined the sea. The road turned into a tarmac path and the tarmac path into a dirt track and then I was on the beach. The clouds moved and the moon shone as though a spotlight had been turned on and I saw the wide sweep of sand and beyond this the sea hardly breaking at all as it met the land. I went down on to the beach and began to walk north.

'By the light of the silvery moon,' I sang quietly to myself, and then began to say and finally to shout:

> *'Tomorrow night, when Phoebe doth behold*
> *Her silver visage in the wat'ry glass*
> *Decking with liquid pearl the bladed grass.'*

I stopped and sobbed. I could hear Philip as Lysander say those lines but it was over now, that dream was over, I would never be Hermia, our *Midsummer Night's Dream* would never be staged. He would know about me now, know that I did not live in a big house in the country, know that I did not have a cousin at RADA, know everything. I thought that he might not mind the lies so much, but knew that he would never allow himself to forgive the make-believe. I imagined him saying 'I told you so'. I sat down behind a breakwater and let myself cry.

Flora was once more at her easel. This was an even older Flora. I knew straight away that she was painting over the original picture. Elizabeth came into the room. She was dressed as though she had been digging in the garden, her shirt sleeves rolled up, her slacks slightly muddy.

'I'm almost finished,' Flora said.

Elizabeth went to look at the painting and grimaced.

'Oh dear!' she said wryly. 'And I thought that I hadn't changed all that much! How the mirror lies.'

Flora stopped painting.

Elizabeth put out her hand and gently ran her finger around Rosie's curls.

Flora began to clean her brushes.

'But what about David?' I asked. I knew that I would not get an answer but nevertheless I repeated, 'Flora, what about David? You've repainted him but you haven't made him old enough, have you?'

Flora continued to whisk the brushes in the cleaning fluid.

'I don't think that I can manage on my own much longer,' Elizabeth said. 'I don't think that the plants want to be here.'

Swish went the paint brushes.

'The maze is getting overgrown. Come and see.'

I stood at the window and watched as they walked away. I found that I was running after them. They went into the darkness of the maze.

David had told the bees that he was going to look after Caffelmeade so why was he not here?

'Where is David?' I shouted.

There was something wrong with my legs. They were tired yet tirelessly thrashed about. They ached but could find no resting place. I longed for stillness but my feet kept moving as though on a treadmill, going constantly but going nowhere. I woke and knew that I had cried out. My voice seemed still to rest on the wind, 'Where are you, Philip?'

It was too cold to sleep again even in the shelter of the breakwater. I flexed my fingers and rubbed my feet. I shivered, but with a deeper cold, a cold that told me that my imagination was failing, flickering like a candle, and would soon be dead. I could walk. I could walk along the beach in the moonlight, I could walk all night if need be and then start for Alnwick at dawn. I did not want to walk the roads in the dark because cars might stop, drivers might offer me a lift, I might even run into a patrolling police car.

I spent an hour on a bench in a shelter. It was under a light and I could see to read. The book in my pocket was getting very shabby and was long overdue at the library. I tried to be interested in the travels of a man who had gone to Brazil in search of orchids, but I was not. I tried just reading the words out loud, not listening to their meaning, just their sound, but it did not work. I tried repeating botanical names, chanting them like a mantra, but it was useless. They were all going away. I had to get to Caffelmeade while there was still a chance. A chance of what? I shied away from that question. Just get to Caffelmeade. Just keep that in mind.

When I gained the dirt track they were there. One second I was alone and the next I was not.

Two came beside me, taking an arm each, and three barred my way. I looked back. There were more behind. A bag was pulled down over my head and although I had just glimpsed them I knew that they were big and unfriendly. By squinting down my nose I could see a thin slice of my arm and the hand that held it. The fingers were inexpertly tattooed at the base as though a pin had been used and the nails were long, pointed and painted in some very dark colour, black or graphite or dried-blood red. Girls, big, well-muscled girls, and they were dragging me off the track. In just a few minutes they had removed my rucksack and my coat, had pulled my sweater down to pinion my arms and pushed me into a ditch. I was not able to protect myself as I fell down and the side of my face and elbow took the impact. I lay where I fell, breathing shallowly so that the dirty paper bag did not get into my mouth. After a while it went quiet. Slowly I sat up, righted my sweater and removed the bag from my head. They were gone and so was my money and my warm coat.

For a while I sat where I was hardly daring to move my arm. This was not in my plan. I tried to stand and was sick. They had been very efficient. No taunting, no threats, no playing around, just swift business and away. They'd taken everything of use, but they had not wanted the book for it was lying face down in the dirt where they had thrown it. My fingers closed around it. I had not imagined anything like this. They had no right to be there. They were not in the story. I had to pull myself together. I had to get to Caffelmeade.

And I did. The tractor driver let me off at the gates. The horsechestnuts had gone, the drive lined with rows of freshly sawn-off stumps. For some reason I thought of Brownies. They looked like stepping stones, a path winding to the house like the Yellow Brick Road. I saw the telltale board and started to run but I knew before I got close enough to read it that Caffelmeade was for sale. The house was boarded up. I went along beside the ten foot high wall made of ancient crumbling brick looking for the painted door. What I found was a neat wrought iron gate. I went through the gate and found myself on a short gravel path.

The path had almost disappeared beneath a carpet of strawberry creepers, and clumps of coarse grass had grown through the gravel. There was a trail of fresh earth in mounds where a mole had scrabbled up for air. The edging stones gleamed with wicked green moss. Michaelmas daisies bloomed in the border, but so did daffodils, and dahlias and hollyhocks as though it was spring and summer and autumn at the same time.

The flowers were noisy. The beds whispered as I approached, murmured as I passed and screamed as they fell behind me. I began to run to get away from the tumult, the clamour as they called for my attention. I came to the rose garden, heavy with scent. Look at me, the rose of York seemed to say. No, look at me, the Lancastrian rose wheedled, think of me, create me.

I had run and run and could run no more. Then I was on my knees beside the dragon. Lichen had eaten away the glaze and small ferns were growing in the empty basin.

'I am Annice Campbell,' I said aloud. 'I am sure of this. I know this, although I am not sure where I am or even when I am. What do I know for certain? I know that tears are running down over my hot cheeks stinging my upper lip.'

I could smell the roses.

'I can't look at you all the time!' I shouted and fled.

The smoke rose behind me, black and acrid.

'You can't call an accident spiteful.'

I ran unheeding into the stove house and the heat descended upon me. My hair hung damply about my face and sweat ran between my shoulder blades inside my elbows and behind my knees. The pitcher plants waved bulbously above me and I blundered out and sank against the wall of the house. I shivered as tendrils of Virginia creeper wrapped themselves around my ankles, twisted over my arms and began to find their way round my neck.

'Get off, you filthy thing!' I yelled and it withered away, first shrinking and then disappearing without trace. A dank, rotting stench came from the open door of the stove house. *Miaow!* I froze and then I was off again, running through the orchard where the trees were in both blossom and fruit. I fell at the greenhouse where the borage burst through the windows, filled the guttering and even blossomed on the roof. I found that I could not get up and dragged myself towards the wheelchair which stood ready outside the stove house. The ground was covered with the spiky balls of winter

157

aconite, but these were hard and razor sharp, cutting my fingers and knees.

'Cruel.'

I dragged myself into the wheelchair. It whizzed through the door of the stove house and began, without my help, to roll towards the pool. I put my hands on the wheels to stop it but it was no good. It purred quietly and inexorably towards the *amazonica*. I saw a flash of pink in the water and covered my face with my hands. The chair stopped on the brink of the pool and I looked down between my feet into the brown water and my shaky reflection. My legs were a tartan of bruises, scratches, and cuts and my left arm looked odd. It was probably broken. I am Annice Campbell!

I struggled out of the chair. I must find the dove tree. Through the beeches I stumbled hearing the voices of Flora and David in my head, 'It is called the handkerchief tree and also the ghost tree.'

At the steep bank I fell and let myself roll. There was no one at the bottom to brush the leaves away from my face.

Flora, Elizabeth, and Matt were walking around the garden for the last time. The 'For Sale' signs were up. Matt was wearing the black jeans from the later painting and he was deeply sun-tanned. He put his arms round both their shoulders.

'Saying goodbye is never easy,' he said. 'But I've done it once and I can do it again.'

They turned into the maze. I followed them. They were going away and if I did not ask them now I would never know. They were always in sight, waiting for me at each turn yet however hard I ran I did not catch up with them.

'Where is David?' I shouted to their backs.

They went on walking.

'What happened to David?' I called again.

They went on walking.

Then a voice in my head said, 'Come on, Annie, this is silly. You know that you can decide for yourself what happened to David. Think. Take control. This is your story. You can do what you want. Maybe he was killed tragically while reaching for a rare mountain plant in the Himalayas? Perhaps he caught some disease while searching for a *bromeliad* in South America and died palely and romantically? But then, perhaps he's not dead at all. Perhaps he and Flora never did get married? No. That was wrong. F. Bennett. She was Flora Bennett so they must have got married. Well then, perhaps it did not work out and they parted. Perhaps he's a lab assistant now in Liverpool. All you have to do, Annie, is choose.'

'But I don't want to,' I sobbed aloud. 'I don't want to make it up. I want to know!'

I turned a corner and they were gone. I blundered on deeper into the maze. The hedges were now more than six feet high, the tops jagged, uncut, and the sides had grown out so that they almost touched across the path. I kept running into dead ends and having to turn back. I had not realized how big the maze was. The Maze. Long Kesh. High security prison. The Maze. The Labyrinth. A labyrinth, and I was not sure what might live in it.

16

If we shadows have offended,
Think but this, and all is mended:
That you have but slumber'd here
While these visions did appear.
A Midsummer Night's Dream, (Act 5, *Scene I*)

I do not know how long I stumbled along the paths,
one arm supporting the other, but I had finally had
enough and at yet another dead end I decided to force
my way through. I got down to ground level where there
seemed to be a bit of space and started to wriggle in. In
spite of the pain I had managed to get my good arm and
most of my shoulders into the hedge, but not through
because it was too wide and too dense. Then I heard the
voices. They were close enough to hear but they were not
in the maze.

'I knew no good would come of it,' Philip said. 'I
said so, didn't I? Play-acting's dangerous. Writers should
be banned. They're not nice people.'

'Hey, it's your fault!'

That sounded like Heather.

'Why me?'

'All that nonsense about snapping back and forth
between time zones. You and your hyperthings!'

'Hyperstrings.'

The voices were dying away, going further into the
garden. It did not matter because they could not really
be there. Heather and Philip were in Manchester.

I gave up trying to get through the hedge and stumbled on. A corner. Another corner. I had reached the centre of the maze. For a moment I thought that I saw the Wolsingtons just as I had seen them that first time, Elizabeth in the white dress, Flora reading and tapping her sandal on David's shoulder, Matt clipping the hedge, and Rosie with the cat and her daisy chain. I blinked and they were gone. Then I thought that I could hear Heather, Sam, and Philip and, most odd of all, Heather's Great-Aunt Madge. I closed my eyes and sank to the grass.

'I'm sorry, but I'll have to sit down for a bit,' Aunt Madge said. It sounded as though they were quite close.

'You don't think that she's here, do you?' Philip challenged.

'I don't know, but I've just driven you at eighty miles an hour up the M62 and the old Ford is a bit noisy, and I'm a bit tired.'

'What about you, Heather?'

'I don't care.'

'Why not?' That was Sam.

'Well, why should I? She lied to us. She told us that she lived in the country in a house with a big garden and that her mother was writing a gardening book, and all the time she lived in Chapman Street and the woman that she said was her mother's secretary is really her mother. She even invented a little sister! So why should I believe it when you tell me that she thought that she could step into a painting? She could have been lying about that too!'

'And you've never made anything up, I suppose?' Aunt Madge asked.

'No,' Heather said.

'What about Pooky?'

'That was different!'

'I don't see how! You had your imaginary friend Pooky for years. We had to set a place for him at table and take him on holiday. Remember when you left him behind at Blackpool and we had to drive back for him?'

'I was only five, for heaven's sake! Anyway, why're you making excuses for her? She was new and strange and we looked after her and she lied to us.'

'She dreamed a few dreams, that's all. And maybe she started to believe them. Dreams are like bottled wishes, but it's best to keep the cork in.'

'Well, we've looked,' Sam said, 'and she's not here.'

'It was always a long shot,' Aunt Madge agreed. 'We wouldn't have found the house if that woman in the post office hadn't known about Frederick Bennett's paintings and just which house we were looking for.'

Frederick? I tried to understand what she was saying. The painter was someone called Frederick? I would have laughed if I could. It was not Flora after all. I had not even got that right! Frederick Bennett! It was funny. It was very funny!

So, I thought, the people in the paintings, Frederick's paintings, may have been real people with real lives, they may even have had lives very like the ones I imagined, but equally, they may not. They may never have existed. They may have been figments of the painter's imagination. The garden at Caffelmeade had certainly fallen into a wilderness, but I did not know why. It did not seem to matter any more.

'But when she does turn up,' I heard Aunt Madge say, 'at least she'll know that you tried. It will show her that she doesn't need to invent things, that she's all right as she is. I feel rested. I think that we can go on now.'

I lifted my head from the ground and tried to call

out. I knew that I was imagining their voices but I still tried to call. My voice hardly sounded at all. I coughed and tried again. Still little more than a hoarse whisper.

> *Lysander! What, remov'd? Lysander, lord!*
> *What, out of hearing? Gone? No sound? No word?*

'Just a minute,' Philip said. 'I think I know where she is. I think that she's in there.'

'The maze?' Aunt Madge asked. 'But it's overgrown. Nobody could get in there.'

'She's in there!'

'Why are you so sure?'

'It was on the postcard and it started me thinking about pattern puzzles. Did you know that 1991 was the Year of the Maze?'

'I did not.'

'What's that got to do with it?' Heather asked.

'Nothing. But as I said, I got interested. It was to celebrate three hundred years since the planting of the great maze at Hampton Court, but they only chose that year because it was the same backwards and forwards. It was a puzzle number. Nothing to do with the planting of the maze at all.'

'So?'

'So I think that there's no point in asking how I know she would come here, because there's no answer. If we want a pattern we have to impose it ourselves.'

'That's not a reason!'

Then Philip shouted, 'All right! I haven't got a reason! I just know she's in there, that's all!'

I am in here, Philip. I am. I am Annice Campbell. I am sure of this. I know this. I have not done anything so very bad. All I have done is invent a few people.

I opened my eyes and David stood before me. He smiled, turned, and walked away.

'David!' I called frantically. 'Philip!'

'Sam,' I heard Philip say, 'she's got to be in there! I have to find her! I have to tell her that I was wrong!'

'You? Wrong? That's a first!' Heather mocked.

'You can't go hacking your way through there,' Aunt Madge said kindly. 'If she's in there she'll hear us.'

'Annice!' she called.

'Annie!'

'Annie!'

'Annice!'

The voices called to me. Oh, if only they were real!

'We'd best start back,' Aunt Madge said. 'We've done our best.'

'Sam, I'm going in,' Philip said. 'I have to tell her that we need to dream, we should dream, we have to dream. Someone's dreams got us out of caves, someone's dreams got us to the moon, someone's dreams will get us to the stars. Everything begins in someone's mind.'

And then I truly knew. I knew that I had always been in charge. I had had a choice as we all have a choice. Every person always has, and always has had, the freedom to choose how they see the world. What I understood for the first time was that we make the world by sifting what we see, feel, hear, read; choosing some of it, rejecting some of it. I knew then that I had to judge what is true. It is up to me.

And now they are in the maze. Philip says, 'If it's the same pattern as Hampton Court, we go left, then right, right, left, left, left, left.'

'I am Annice Campbell. I know where I am, I know when I am, and I know that my real friends are coming to find me.'

They are here and Heather says gruffly, 'And a fine mess you've got yourself into!'

Aunt Madge bends to look at me.

'A broken arm, but otherwise nothing that a night's sleep and a plate of egg and chips won't cure. Can you stand? We could carry you out between us.'

'I'm walking out of here on my own two feet,' I say.

'I knew you were here,' Philip says to me.

'I know you did.'

'Come on then,' Aunt Madge says. 'Have you forgotten? *The Dream?* I don't think Miss Ogle can read all the parts. You've a play to put on!'

In the garden, new growth is shooting from the base of the dead tree, new leaves and one white handkerchief.

Mrs Campbell closed the book. *Naturalists both Amateur and Mercenary*. It seemed to her both harmless and dull, but it had been neither for Annie.

The trouble with books, she thought, is that books change people. The trouble is that you are never quite the same person at the end of a book as you were at the beginning and writers know this.

She purposely left the book on the park bench and walked home.

Up in her attic Annie was sitting at the word processor. She was writing a story.

'I am Annice Campbell. I am sure of this . . .'

As her fingers wandered over the keys she was watching her fictional characters dance, and was waiting to see what they would do.

Other Oxford fiction

The War Orphan
Rachel Anderson
ISBN 0 19 275095 X

'You can't say anything can you? You know nothing. You are nothing.
You are a dot. You are one of a hundred thousand homeless children.
You are just a casualty of war.'

Once Simon had thought he was in control of his life. But what
is the story he keeps hearing in his head? Is it his own? Or does
it belong to the child who his parents claim is his brother—Ha,
the war orphan?

Simon is becoming obsessed by the fascination, the horror, and
all engulfing reality of total war.

The Scavenger's Tale
Rachel Anderson
ISBN 0 19 275022 4

It is 2015, after the great Conflagration, and London has
become a tourist sight for people from all over the world,
coming to visit the historic Heritage Centres. These are out of
bounds to people like Bedford and his sister Dee who live in
an Unapproved Temporary Dwelling and have to scavenge
from skips and bins just to stay alive.

Bedford begins to notice something odd about the tourists:
when they arrive in the city, they are desperately ill, but when
they leave they seem to have been miraculously cured. And
then the Dysfuncs start disappearing. It is only when a stranger
appears, terribly injured, that Bedford begins to put two and
two together . . .

Sweet Clarinet
James Riordan
Shortlisted for the 1998 Whitbread Children's Award
ISBN 0 19 275050 X

Billy thinks growing up in wartime is fun—falling bombs, fiery skies. That is, until a bomb falls on him.

From that moment on, Billy's life will never be the same again. Horribly burned, Billy longs for death—but the precious gift he receives might just give him something to live for . . . and some hope for the future.

*'A **really** good book'*

Whitbread Judges

The School That Went On Strike
Pamela Scobie
ISBN 0 19 275051 8

'What can you do? Nobody listens to children.'
'Oh, no? Then we'll MAKE them listen! If the grown-ups won't go on strike—WE WILL!'

And that's exactly what Violet and the rest of the pupils at Burston School do. They are fed up with the way their teachers have been treated and decide that there is only one way to make themselves heard . . .

Based on true events, this is the story of a group of children who come together to fight for goodness and justice—it's the story of the school that went on strike.